Only She Knew

A Bindarra Creek Mystery Romance

Linda Charles

Contents

Chapter One

"*Found you!*"
    Jennifer Rogers stared at the message scrawled in white paint across her employer's company car. The graffiti all but obscured the new branding he'd spent the past few months designing. Laurie had loaned her the car yesterday so she'd drop off the "Open House" signs on her way to work. She dropped her bag and ran to the damaged car. Her good mood vanished in a blink. What did it mean? "*Found you!*"

She touched the white paint but it was long dry. Why would pranksters or vandals be prowling about her family's property late at night? And it was weird she hadn't heard anything. Her bedroom faced the driveway. An engine would have drawn attention.

Jen scanned the nearby paddocks, her body quivering. The message could be meant for her boss, Laurie. He was loud, opinionated and known to speak his mind. It might explain the graffiti, as their property, Whispering Mist, was only twenty minutes out of town. But she couldn't recall being followed home last night, and from the road nobody would see the car.

"Dad!" she yelled. "Dad! Come out here."

In a nearby paddock two of her father's horses raised their heads and looked in her direction. She turned around and swore under her breath. The same ugly words were scrawled across her father's ute and the wooden shed.

"Dad!"

The screen door of the house flew open. Her father stepped onto the verandah; his loose comfortable clothing hid the wiry muscle-hardened body of a jockey. His gaze shifted from her to the car and in an instant his face sagged.

Her mother appeared in the doorway, still dressed in her floral pyjamas, and drying her hands with a kitchen towel. "Oh, John, who would do such a thing?"

"Your guess is as good as mine," he said as he descended the steps.

Her mother pushed her glasses higher on her nose and followed. "Maybe it's a punter who lost at the track?"

Her father shook his head and walked to his ute. "I doubt it, Pam, no country punter would do something like this. It'll be someone with a gripe against Jen's boss."

Jen felt her mother's arm come around her waist. "You take my car this morning, Jen, and let your father and me sort this out."

"Thanks, Mum, but Laurie will want to see the damage. He'll need to get it assessed. Oh god, insurance - we've only just sent the paperwork through."

"Calm down, love," her father urged. "It's not your fault."

"I know that." Jen flexed her hands in an effort to control her growing frustration. The timing sucked big time. Two days ago, Laurie had made the surprise announcement to promote her from the reception desk to showing properties on a Saturday. Her hopes and dreams of working with Laurie Chester and the chance to be made a permanent member of staff were tied up in that car. "This is a new car, Dad. We only picked it up yesterday."

"I'll get something to clean the paint off my ute." Her father marched towards the shed.

The front screen door slammed hard against the side of the house. Jen's Aunt JoJo stood in the doorway, clutching Cleopatra, her latest favourite doll against her chest. At sixty her father's older sister no longer bore any resemblance to the woman whose photo, taken at her debutante ball, once graced the shop front of the local photographer for months. Jen couldn't remember a time when JoJo hadn't lived with them.

"What's happening?" asked JoJo.

"Someone's been up to mischief," Jen's mother announced.

Mischief? Someone's broken the law. Jen looked at the car again. Her stomach clenched every time she read *Laurie Chester's Realty*, with only *Laurie* and *Realty* left partly unscathed. "Dad, we should call the police. They would be on top of things like this and know of any new trouble-makers in town."

Her mother patted her arm. "Onto it, love, I'll get your father's mobile and we'll take some shots before you go."

Jen's father emerged from the shadows of the shed waving his mobile. "Leave it, Pam. I'll do it now before Jen sets off."

Jen stared out at the paddocks. Whispering Mist was the only home she'd ever known and this graffiti was such an invasion it shocked her to the core. She doubted she'd ever sleep well in her bed again or feel safe. Whoever had done this had stood only a few metres from her room.

A long painful wail sliced through the air.

Jen turned at the familiar sound and saw JoJo on the other side of the car. Horror filled her as her aunt sank to the stone-pebbled ground. With one arm still clutching Cleopatra to her chest, JoJo raised a shaking finger and pointed to the car.

Jen ran to her stricken aunt. Jen slid to the ground and wrapped her arms around her aunt's frail frame and gently rocked and crooned to the frightened woman. JoJo never moved. Her eyes were fixed ahead. Jennifer's heart lost a beat as she read the words splashed across Laurie's sign.

Where are the jewels?????

"What the hell is this?"

Her mother came around the car, worry etched across her face. "What?"

"Look at it, Mum. It says "where are the jewels?" Is this some kind of sick joke?"

Her mother stared at the graffiti. Pam's hands flew to the thin gold chain around her neck. "It has to be. There are no jewels here."

Her mother joined her and together they helped JoJo to her feet.

Her father came forward, his frown deepening as he stared at the graffiti. He put an arm around Pam's shoulder. "Pam, stop it. We both know what this is about."

Her father's words silenced them all.

Jen bit her bottom lip as she processed this revelation.

"I don't know what this is about." Jen piped up. "Will somebody tell me?"

Her father spoke, his speech unrushed and clear. "Well before you were born, about thirty years ago, JoJo and your Uncle Stan owned a jewellery store in town. Three of our shearers that year robbed them. They took off with the cash and jewels after they'd bashed Stan."

Jen's mind churned through past conversations, sifting through hints and whispers. "Uncle Stan? I thought he died young of a heart attack. I never heard of him being bashed."

JoJo whimpered, her hands grabbing at her mother's arms. Her mother turned and looked at Jen for a minute seeming stricken at the current discussion.

Her father ran a hand through his hair. "He died of a heart attack a couple of hours after the bashing. Any mention of him upsets JoJo, so it's never mentioned. Go to work, love, we'll discuss it later."

Hurt and disappointment cascaded through her.

How could she concentrate at work when someone was stalking them? Did her parents really think she could go to work as if nothing had happened when everything had changed? Questions, so many questions whipped around her brain at breakneck speed. She struggled to maintain her self-control.

She stood her ground. "Why, Dad? What do they mean by "found you"? And what's with "where are the jewels?" Who announces they're looking for stolen loot?"

"I've no idea, love," he said. His soft raspy voice reeked of a weariness that tugged at her heart.

Jen's head was spinning with questions. "What happened to the robbers? Were they ever caught?"

Her mother grimaced. "Stop it, stop hounding your father."

"No, they were never caught." Her father answered.

Jen circled around the car. "This could get nasty. You and Mum live a cloistered life out here. In town, there's the odd theft and there's quite a few newbies in Bindarra Creek these days. I'm just saying it could be an outsider who's heard the story. They get hammered at the pub and someone talks and one thing leads to another."

Her father raised his eyebrows and her mother shot her "the look".

Jen held up her hand. "Sorry, Dad. I don't mean to be alarmist, but somebody is threatening us. I see this as a veiled threat."

"Nobody we know would do this to us." Her father's quietly spoken words stilled her.

She let out a soft groan. "I hate to tell you, Dad, but gone are the days when you knew everyone in town. Bindarra Creek is growing."

Her mother tapped her frail aunt on the arm. "Come on, JoJo. Forget about this, somebody's stirring up trouble. Let's go inside and have a nice cuppa, eh?"

Jen caught her mother's eye. Her mother's resigned expression tore at her. With JoJo's dementia worsening, they both knew this incident might trigger an outburst later today.

Together Jen and her mother helped JoJo climb the stairs. Jen reached out and gave her mother and JoJo each a kiss on the cheek. "I need to head off."

She picked up her bag from where she'd dropped it on the verandah, pulled out her phone and took a few shots of the damaged vehicle.

Jen paced alongside the front of the car in an effort to compose herself before she called her boss. She sat on the bottom step, took a deep breath and hit his number.

"Laurie," she cut in before he said a word. "There's some graffiti on your car. Someone did it overnight." The words were out, rushed and tumbled, but it didn't ease her growing anxiety.

"Much damage?"

"Yes, both sides. All the doors need a complete re-spray. I'm so sorry, I don't know who's done this."

Laurie let out a deep sigh. "Here's what you'll do. Run the car down to Reg's old place, you know it?"

Who didn't know the dusty old eyesore just past Kingfisher Bridge? "Yes, but it's been empty for years."

"Not anymore. Reg's leased it out to two brothers and I'm sure they do spray painting out the back. I know they've jazzed up a second hand go-kart for one of the neighbors' kids. I'm sure one of those boys did it."

Jen stood up, anxious to get started on fixing the car. "Good," said Jen. "I'll run it down now."

"We might be in luck if they can do a quick turn around on this for us."

"Thanks, Laurie. I'll see what I can do."

"Jen, one more thing." Laurie's voice boomed into her ear. "Don't forget to haggle, see if they'll negotiate on the price."

"Right, I'll try. Laurie. I'll see you later."

Jennifer swallowed down her dismay. Her day was slowly going down the gurgler. What new guys in town?

Her father stood by Laurie's car. She went up to him and gave him a quick hug. "All good with Laurie. You call the police?"

He nodded. "I'll ring them as soon as I go inside."

Jen settled into Laurie's car relishing the quiet, the coolness and the peace. She waved to her father then plopped her open bag on the seat beside her. After switching on the engine, she reached inside her bag and pulled out half a dozen jellybeans. She popped one into her mouth.

Her mind buzzed at the thought of missing jewels and her family's possible involvement. She couldn't wait to run a search at work to find out more.

She eased her foot off the brake and let the car roll down the driveway. With fresh eyes she studied each paddock and building.

Was someone out there watching?

Chapter Two

Jen reached into her bag and popped a jelly bean into
her mouth.

She needed to collect her thoughts. Laurie had im-
pressed her with his decency. He'd put in plans for the new
branding six months ago and had worked hard to prepare
for their in-house Q&A sessions and the impressive cat-
alogue of homes to show. They all knew how important
this long weekend meant to him and the business.

Her mind switched into gear as she drove to the garage.
Something didn't sit well with her when she thought
about two new guys in town. The old garage was diag-
onally opposite the Riverside pub, on the other side of
Kingfisher Bridge. They had to drive past it to get in and
out of town. When Reg's place was a going concern, every
Friday night his guys went to the Riverside after work.
Most people she knew did. Reg still did.

Perhaps Laurie was right, and she did walk around with
blinkers on. Not anymore. Sometime last night someone
had crossed the line and attached her family. They'd put

her family on notice that things were about to change. *Found you!* Who would do this to her family? If it was related to the robbery, why now, after all these years? What was so significant about now?

Jen turned her thoughts to the task ahead. But haggling with a mechanic, a total stranger, over the price of the re-spray paint job frightened the life out of her. If she couldn't do that, how would she ever tell an expectant seller they couldn't expect the high price they wanted? She sighed. What use was Jen to Laurie's business if she couldn't deal with the hard stuff? Therein lay the rub.

She drove slowly over Kingfisher Bridge and eyed the old garage. She couldn't see any change. It still looked dusty, dirty and abandoned.

As she approached it nervous flutters pinched her stomach. She eased her foot on the brake before she turned left, and drove into the carpark.

She looked about, but couldn't see any sign of life, or movement. Tall flowering weeds infested the cracks between the broken cement slabs of the carpark. To her left stood the old wooden workshop and the sign above, *Kingfisher Garage*, hung lopsided above the door. An old flag, now tattered and threadbare fluttered in the breeze just outside the driveway as it had done for years.

What is going on here? It looked as though someone had shut the door and walked away. She sat with the motor running, unsure of what to do.

She leaned forward and scanned down the side of the building. Lined up by the old wooden fence were a few badly rusted cars, each with a heavy cloth covering them. Nothing new there.

Still, no movement.

Across from the garage sat a smaller building, the office, and the small cement path leading to it looked as though it had been swept. *That's something.* She wound down her window but couldn't hear a sound.

She could almost hear Laurie say the old buildings oozed potential. And they did. Granted they needed a lot of work, but with a good lick of paint and a few things repaired Jen could see possibilities. Its location, just outside the city centre and on the main road to Moree could not be bettered.

Curious, and against her better judgement, she shut down the engine, opened the door and stepped out. She slammed her door shut and heard a series of barks - deep warning barks.

With one hand on the door handle Jen waited for activity. Where there are dogs there are people, handlers, and owners. She hoped they weren't too far away. As a country girl she wasn't afraid of dogs, but there was a certain layer to this dog's bark which set her nerves on edge.

Then she heard it, a flurry of footsteps, which grew louder.

"Hey, it's okay. He's only a pup."

She turned and saw an adorable black and tan pup run toward her at full speed.

That bark did not come from this dog.

The excited pup jumped up against her legs. She bent down at the same time it bounced up and its head hit the bottom of her chin. The bundle of fur kept running around her feet, then jumping up one leg at a time. Its hot breath brushed across her face. Time and time again it squirmed out of Jen's reach.

The pup jumped a little away from her, and stopped, cocking its head as it stared at her. She grabbed its paws.

"Gotcha," she cried out.

Wet.

Jen dropped its paws in horror. Her hands were wet and muddy and she shook them in an effort to get them dry.

"Get down, Jasper. Now."

Jasper paused for a split second and ignored his owner. Jasper leaned in closer to her, his dark snout sniffing out her pockets. She tried to push him down, but his confused dark brown eyes zeroed in on her, and his doggy charm started to work its magic.

Then two arms reached down and held him in place. In front of her a blond guy put a leash on the quick-as-a-whippet squirming puppy.

The guy had muscles, some serious muscle power. Jen studied the bulging muscles of his bare arms, and all the ones that ran down his back, which were housed in the tightest t-shirt and jeans.

Gym junkie.

He stood up and faced her, his blue eyes shining bright in his suntanned face, as did his infectious smile. Jen found the combination hard to resist, and she smiled back.

The guy's eyes roved over her body and then his face screwed up - not the usual response when some guy checked her out. He nodded to her front.

She followed his gaze. Several dirty damp patches of mud were on her stomach and thighs. Jen brushed at the worst patches on her pants, but as her hands kept brushing the patches widened.

Jen groaned.

A male hand, sporting a few cuts and a couple of white flecks of dried paint, brushed hers aside. "Wait a bit. It's best to wait for them to dry out, and then brush off the dust."

She pursed her lips. Great, now she looked like an idiot in front of Gym Junkie.

Jen straightened. "Thanks. I'm just in a rush; it's been a busy day already."

The office door flew open with a bang and another fair-haired guy poked his head out of the building. He waved from the office door and strode toward them, his eyes taking in the graffiti on Jen's car.

As he approached, his lips curled into a welcome smile. His smart clothing - jeans and an open-necked shirt - fitted him like a glove. His long and slender figure and well-cut hair matched his groomed appearance.

He's dapper.

Dapper held out a hand and she shook it, receiving a firm shake in return.

Jen stared at the two good-looking men. The brothers - so obvious with the same fair hair, square jaw, blue eyes - would stand out in any crowd. *Why haven't Taylah and I seen them about?* She couldn't help but wonder what they were doing working out of Reg's old garage.

Dapper raised an eyebrow. "I see Jasper's left you a couple of his love patches."

She laughed it off. "No permanent damage. I'm actually here on business. Are you open? Do you spray paint?" She waved her arms over the damaged car. "See my problem? My boss would love this little problem remedied as soon as."

Gym Junkie stood back as Dapper stepped forward. "We sure do."

"That's great," she said, hearing her obvious relief lacing her voice. "Yeah, some idiot had a go about something. Can you do this? Give me a price?"

Dapper walked around her car, studying it and nodding. "Sure can. So he wants the brand back shiny and bright?" He ran his hand over the damage. "Jewels?" He shot her a brief smile. "Did you break a heart?"

At the suggestive way he said "break a heart", Jen blushed, big time. She touched her face. Her cheeks were burning hot.

He gave her a quick short nod. "Okay. Four grand and we can start on it today."

Jen lurched. "Four grand?"

She bit her bottom lip and wondered how to start haggling. "Is that the best you can do?"

Gym Junkie stepped forward. For the briefest moment, something akin to interest flickered in his eyes, then disappeared. A sliver of hope slithered down her spine, he seemed the more practical of the pair.

"We can do it for two grand, five hundred a panel, if you leave it here now. I can run you into town and start on it today. I don't think your boss would like his damaged car paraded around town, do you?"

Dapper raised an eyebrow, and something about his disapproval disappointed her, but he didn't say anything.

Relief shunted through her - she could live with that. "Could you? Oh, that'd be great. Thank you so much."

Jen's glance flickered across to Dapper, the one who she suspected called the shots in this operation, but he remained expressionless.

Gym Junkie didn't notice. He pursed his lips, as if holding back on a smile, and after a beat he nodded. "We have a deal. Two grand it is."

Jen ignored the stifled snort from Dapper.

She stared into the Gym Junkie's eyes, the deepest blue she'd ever seen, and held out her hand. "Oh, that's great. Thank you so much."

He stepped forward, positioning his rock-hard body between Jen and Dapper. He reached out and took her hand in his. Her eyes flew down at their hands in her surprise and delight at the sudden warmth and comfort from his large, solid hand shake.

Laurie sprang to mind, which spurred her into action. Jen ran around to the driver's side of the car, snatched her bag and fumbled with the junk inside until she found a few business cards. She grabbed two of them.

As she walked back to the two men, Jen couldn't help but notice their size. She slowed her pace, very aware of their height and build. As a unit they had quite a presence and the air around them seemed to throb with their raw masculinity.

She handed each of them a card. "I should introduce myself. I'm Jennifer Rogers - call me Jen, everybody does. I work at *Laurie Chester's Realty* on Main Street in town. If ever you're looking for a place to rent or buy, we're onto it. Please call me if you need anything."

Dapper took her card, and turned it over in his hand. "Thanks. Good to know. I'm Gareth Colder." His eyes shot to his brother. "And he's Brock."

***

Brock Colder pulled back and held firm against a bored and frustrated Jasper who hadn't given up and kept wrenching hard against its lead in an effort to get free and play.

Jennifer Rogers stood waiting before him. An expectant expression on her lovely face jolted him back to reality. "Give me a minute and I'll get my keys. We'll go in my suv and I'll run you back into town."

She smiled at him. "Thank you. I really appreciate it."

Brock slapped his brother on the shoulder. "Come on, let's go in and sort these keys. Won't be long."

Once inside the privacy of their hot and dusty workshop, Gareth punched his fist into the air and then ran and jumped onto an empty workbench. He sat on the bench, sheer joy beaming across his face.

Gareth punched the air again. "Holy hell, things couldn't get any better. How the hell did we manage that? We cause the damage and then we get paid to repair it. I swear there's a business model in there somewhere. God, I'm so slow on these things sometimes. It's worth thinking about."

Ignoring his brother, Brock took Jasper out to the small enclosed backyard and released him to join his mother, T-Rex. Not for the first time he wondered if his brother missed out on an empathy gene.

Back inside he refrained from responding to Gareth's smug expression as he headed to the side wall and picked up his suv's keys.

Gareth grinned. "It's worth a thought. My mind's exploding right now with possibilities. Do you realise we have a small army of would-be could-be's back in Tamworth? A call is all it would take and a couple of guys one night a week, splashing a bit of paint around, breaking a few car lights. Nothing major, it's bread and butter work. It brings in the type of money flow that keeps a business in operation."

Brock stared at his brother. "Drop it. Stop thinking like that. We're here for another month, that's it."

Gareth kept grinning at him. "This is going to work. You being so friendly and all, working your obvious charm you'll worm your way into her family. It doesn't get any better. Unbelievable! We can search that property anytime, and she'll be none the wiser. Clueless."

Brock ran a hand through his hair. He'd promised his brother one month, and then they'd go their separate ways. Thirty one days in October. Thirty to go.

His brother's twisted joy sickened him.

Their father had always pitted them one against the other. In his final twisted, loving act, he sent them on some half-assed search and rescue mission to find their so-called inheritance.

Gareth had leapt at the chance to get away and start afresh. The money would help finance his new start in Sydney.

Brock wasn't convinced. He doubted his father's final words. Most things spouted from that man's mouth were questionable. After months of pleading, bargaining and downright arguing, his brother had worn him down, and he'd given in to Gareth's outrageous plans.

Today hit him hard.

Not once did he think of the very real consequences of what they were doing. At no point did he think they'd be hurting anybody.

Jen Rogers, as cute as, made him feel bad. She was a direct consequence of their dirty deeds last night. Here she was rocking up asking for help for the damage they'd caused. He'd caused this to someone, an innocent someone. Taking her back to the office would be a challenge and he was no actor.

He could hear Gareth saying she was collateral damage and not to worry about it. But he did worry about it.

Brock stepped out into the backyard. He pulled down his shades in the bright sunlight, and spotted Jen standing in the far corner of the property. Dressed in a fitted black pant suit and bright blue shirt she looked a real honey.

She waved him over and he joined her.

"What plans do you have for this place?" she asked.

Plans? That word did not enter his world. Nobody in his family lived by plans, they lived by moods. When things got a little too difficult, or work slowed down, as it often did, they moved on. He was only marking time till something better, more enticing, even different, came along.

Before he could respond Jen pointed to the old garage shed, a wide grin on her face. "You're standing on a gold mine. This place is a diamond in the rough, a real one."

He shook his head. Another dreamer.

Jen ran out in front of him, her arms extended wide, and she twirled around. "Tell me to shut up if you want to, but this place is crying out with opportunity."

His stomach churned. How he hated that word, opportunity. To him it meant wasted time, dead ends and starting over. He and Gareth had lived with their father while he chased opportunities around the country. It led to more dead ends in his life than hot dinners. As for dreams, he'd start one at each move they made, but then his father would have a change of heart and they'd move on, and another one of his dreams would fall by the wayside.

Brock forced a grin. "What opportunity?"

She threw back her head and laughed out loud. "Can't you see it? Great location, plenty of parking. The old office shed can be turned into a small café; you've got the big garage which will do whatever it is mechanics do in there, and the best part is you can do it all without a reception area. You can wear a small iPad in a pouch, it's like a mobile office where you can check cars in and receive delivery goods - even use it to place orders for cakes and coffees or whatever. You can use the real estate of the reception area to make money for you, rather than be dead real estate doing nothing for you."

Jen ran up to the top of the path. "And the best thing is you're the first business anyone sees coming off Kingfisher Bridge, and you're diagonally opposite the pub, people can see you from there. It's on the way to Moree. As I said, great location."

Brock let the minutes tick by in silence, too surprised for words. He couldn't speak for fear his words would muddy the very real picture Jen had painted.

She rushed up to him, all blonde, bright and bubbly. Cuddly, too. *Forget it*. He couldn't make any connections. He met her gaze for one long moment. "Well," she said breathily, her soft fragrance tantalising him. "What do you think?"

Chapter Three

Jen closed Brock's car door and waved him on after he'd dropped her off at the back of the agency. The guy was the strong silent type. She mused over how he'd allowed her to prattle on about the delights of living in Bindarra Creek. He'd good naturedly nodded at certain intervals.

She searched the carpark and the street for any sign of Laurie's car. No car. Good. She didn't need any distraction from him for a while.

Jen strode down the narrow corridor her mind focused on one thing. In reception sat Melissa, Laurie's sister, his business partner and office manager.

"Morning Mel. When's Laurie back?" Jen asked as she switched on her PC and peeled her blazer off and settled it on the back of her chair. She emptied the last of her jelly beans into a large glass bowl on the corner of her desk and stored away her bag in the bottom drawer of her desk.

Mel swung around and grinned at her. "Hi there, Jen, he should be back in thirty minutes. As usual he stormed out of here."

"Good," said Jen as she clicked onto the local search engine. In the search bar she entered 'jewellery robbery bindarra creek'. She clicked on the first few links but saw nothing that helped her. The fifth link sent her to a story dated Monday, 5 October 1998 in the The Tamworth Herald. She opened it and read:

Brazen Jewellery Robbery in Bindarra Creek

An investigation is underway into a robbery by three men who brazenly broke into a Bindarra Creek jewellery store last week and made off with an estimated $30,000 worth of merchandise, according to the local police.

Jeweller, Stanley Rogers has been transported to Tamworth Hospital after being assaulted during the robbery.

The incident, which involved three local shearers, happened just after 2:30 p.m. local time last Friday afternoon. Locals advise the shearers; Dan Thompson, Alan Colt and Greg Simpson were due to begin their army training in the New Year and were working their way to Sydney.

Witnesses felt the robbery was carefully planned. They reported seeing one man initially standing at the front door of Rogers' Jewellery, a retailer whose shop is located on the busy Main Street in Bindarra Creek.

The trio used crowbars to break open display cases lining the back wall at the store. They pulled items from nearby shelves and shoved them into their bags.

Should anybody have any information, please call Crime Stoppers NSW.

Jen wrote down the names of the shearers. They meant nothing to her. She searched first, Dan Thompson, Alan Colt, and then, Greg Simpson, but couldn't see anything that stood out.

Mel dropped a coffee on her desk. "Everything alright?"

Jen shook her head. "I'm not sure. JoJo and her husband had their jewellery shop robbed about thirty years ago and I'm just curious if there's any mention of it anywhere."

"Wow, did they catch the guys?"

Jen shook her head. "No, and I can't find anything about them, other than their names."

"Try the police," Mel suggested. "They look at cold cases. Try Abby Taylor, she's now Senior Constable."

Jen grabbed a jelly bean and popped it in her mouth. "Thanks, Mel. I'll do that." She grabbed the glass bowl and took it over to Mel. "Help yourself. If I had any more I'll be crawling the walls."

Jen sat back at her desk and studied the names. Is there a connection somewhere? She couldn't tell. Perhaps she was looking for something that didn't exist.

The back door slammed shut.

Damn.

Jen shut down search screen and clicked on to the Profit & Loss page.

***

Hours later Jen waited for the swirl of icy-cold beer to slide down her throat before she slammed her empty glass onto the table. She loved pubs, loved the casualness of them, and there were none better than the Riverside.

Her breathing deepened as the cool ale filtered into her body with the hidden magic to calm every nerve ending. After such a difficult day the cold beer helped in a huge way to take the edge off her stressful day. The Riverside was fast filling up - not bad for a Saturday evening. Maybe she and Taylah should start thinking about getting their dinner order in.

She stretched out, her legs ached after spending a day on her feet. Laurie's marketing plans and tight schedules were beginning to bite.

She mulled over his latest demands. Such an easy request, but he wanted it done yesterday. Somewhere he'd read a book about some marketing guru none of them knew, but he now lived by a new eighty-twenty rule, with eighty percent of his time on work and the other twenty percent on marketing. Somehow she got roped into that marketing sequence. He dreamed up new campaigns, and she and Melissa, were the ones who ran around like headless chooks, making it all happen for him.

She glanced across at her best friend, Taylah McKenna, who was downing the last of her beer.

"I need your help. You doing anything later tonight?"

Taylah's amusement was written all over her face. She stood up and looked around. "Well, Mr Right hasn't rocked up yet, so there's a good chance after dinner I can spare a few hours."

"You're going to wish Mr Right would rush in with what I've got in mind. Laurie's got this new campaign going out and he wants us to put three hundred open house notices into envelopes so they can be posted first thing Monday morning."

Taylah rolled her eyes.

Jen nodded. "I know. He drops that one as he's walking out the door. Nothing new there."

Taylah picked up her empty glass. "I'll get us another beer. Share a pizza?"

Jen agreed then stood up to check out who was in. She waved to a few friends at a table by the bar.

Taylah returned and handed her a cold beer. "Who are you looking for?"

Jen shook her head. "Thanks. No one. Just seeing who's in."

A few tables behind Taylah, Florrie Miller was headed in their direction. In her hands were a book of tickets and a small bag around her waist. "Don't put your wallet, away. Here comes Florrie."

No doubt selling tickets for some charity, mused Jen. She'd known Florrie all her life, and couldn't be more proud of her now she was the newly ordained Church of England vicar.

Jen pulled out her purse in readiness. "Hey Florrie, what's the charity?"

The older woman joined them. Her face was red from the heat in the crowded room. "Well hello, ladies, it's been a while. Okay, tickets are two dollars each and it's to pay for new chairs and tables for the Council's child-care centre. We're getting more and more littlies joining us and we want to brighten the place up a bit."

Jen handed her ten dollars. Every week Florrie sold tickets to raise money for a need nobody else in town really noticed. "Sounds good. Get the tickets from anywhere in your ticket book, thanks, Florrie."

"Me too," echoed Taylah.

Florrie tore the tickets off and handed them to the girls. "Now, what are you two doing here on a Saturday night? It's the long weekend. Aren't there any concerts on somewhere?"

Taylah grimaced. "Not a plan in sight. The long weekend's crept up, besides there's quite a few strangers here tonight."

"Speaking of strangers, I met the two brothers that are working out of Reg's old garage today, and I thought they might be in tonight, but I don't see them. Pity. They're both cute."

Florrie pulled up a chair and joined them. "Oh, I heard Reg had let that out. But, back to you pair. You should be out tonight, at a party or something. You can't sit around and think Mr Right's going to wander in here, and notice you."

Jen laughed out loud. "There's a problem with that. There's a shortage of available men."

Florrie put her tickets in her pouch. "You girls are so fussy. How can you say that? Are you forgetting about the new Army training facility just outside of town?"

Jen clapped her hands. "Oh, good one, Florrie, I forgot about that."

Florrie's eyes twinkled as she grinned at the girls. "In my day we played musical chairs, and if you wound up with some young man on the other side, sometimes he let you win and you tended to stay with him for the rest of the evening. It worked well back in the day."

Taylah leaned in closer. "Is that how you met Jonas?"

Jen caught the glint in Florrie's eyes. "Go on, Florrie, you can tell us."

At that Florrie snapped her bag shut with a cheeky grin plastered across her face. "I'll save that for another day."

Jen watched Florrie move onto the next table, and then sat back to sip her beer. She and Taylah loved to people-watch.

Taylah's phone buzzed and she pulled it out of her back pocket. "When was the last time you checked your phone?"

The tone in Taylah's voice jerked Jen out of her daydream. Taylah stood up, "Come on. Your mother's texted saying JoJo's missing."

Jen followed Taylah out of the pub. Her thoughts centred on JoJo. Over time JoJo's dementia seemed to be getting worse, or maybe slowly evolving into something else. Lately JoJo had taken to running away to the nearest paddock, but she'd always stayed close to home.

***

Thirty minutes later Taylah was driving them up the Rogers' driveway.

From the beginning of the rise, Jen could see the lights on at the old homestead where her father and her Uncle Stan were raised. To the right of that was the old shearing shed, a huge two-storey building now used as a storage shed; it too had all its lights on. Jen couldn't remember the last time she'd seen the homestead so lit up, both inside and outside their home.

Jen fisted her hands in her lap, anxious about her aunt. JoJo rarely left Pam's side; they were almost joined at the hip, plus JoJo was a homebody who never strayed far. What had caused JoJo to run off?

Jen's eyes lifted to the sudden movement on the verandah and saw her mother's anxious face as she stood beside Rosie, Taylah's mother, looking out. Jen's father raced out of the shed and indicated to Jen and Taylah that they stay in the ute and meet him at the top of the driveway.

Both girls wound down their windows, and Jen leaned out as they approached her father.

"Dad, what's happened?" He looked haggard as he leaned against the door frame beside her.

He ran a hand across his tired face. "Hi girls. I don't know what happened. Just before dinner JoJo ran out screaming. Your mother chased after her, toward the old homestead, but fell over half-way down that small track running between the two sheds and lost sight of her. We haven't seen JoJo since," he finished with a groan. His voice laced with exhaustion. Jen wanted nothing more than to wrap her arms about her father, but he wouldn't want that. None of them could rest until they found JoJo. Instead, she laid a hand over her father's and squeezed it. "Have you called the police?"

He shook his head. "Not yet."

"Not yet? Why not, dad?"

"Because I told him not to." Her mother joined them, the breeze playing with her hair. "She can't be far. If she's not found in an hour, we'll call then."

Jen bit her bottom lip. "Okay. Where have you searched?"

Her father's eyes misted. "Everywhere we could think of. We've searched every building twice, both your mothers have walked the paddocks, and I've driven over them with the high beams on a couple of times, but we can't see or hear her. But she can't be far."

"What about our place?" asked Taylah.

Her father gave a quick nod. "Your mother's checked the stables, checked Big Bertha, we know she loves the caravan - and even the dogs were sent into the dams for a swim to see if they found anything. We've searched around our dams, but I don't think JoJo'd go into water."

"Okay," said Taylah. "Where would you like us to go?"

Her father pointed toward the old homestead. "You can try the back paddocks again, maybe down the back lane?"

Jen leaned across and gave her father a quick peck on the cheek. "Try not to worry, Dad. We'll search and honk the horn twice if we find her. Okay?"

Her father pulled away and waved the girls on. "Don't rush it, and have a good look about."

Without another word Taylah put on the ute's high-beams, and they headed towards the old homestead.

Jen looked out the window, into the pitch black and couldn't contain her growing unease. JoJo was in bed most nights by eight o'clock. Why would she run off?

Taylah drove close to the old homestead, but even with the high-beams on, Jen couldn't see any movement.

Jen sat up. "Drop me off here and I'll take a quick look inside."

She climbed out of the ute, and ran across to the old wooden structure. Her heavy footsteps echoed on the loose floorboards of the verandah, and she pushed open the door.

"JoJo!"

She flicked on the light and was hit with a shock of colour. It shouldn't surprise her, but it did every time she walked into the small living room. The Dolls, dressed in every colour imaginable covered all four walls. It was a testament to JoJo's obsession with dolls. Years ago, as her collection grew, her father had built two shelves against each wall, and the room looked spectacular with the dolls all sitting side by side. As a child, Jen had played with JoJo dressing her dolls together, but right now she felt their lifeless eyes upon her.

Everything looked to be in place. To her right sat a small settee for three, a sideboard and a radio sat on top, and on the other side of the room, against the back wall, was a small dining table with four chairs.

Jen shivered. She loved this place, this hidey-hole, but tonight it gave her the creeps.

She strode straight to the small kitchen behind the lounge room. Nothing out of place. She walked down the hall and checked the two back bedrooms and their wardrobes. All empty.

Outside, she walked the circumference of the building, then shook her head to Taylah.

"Nothing," she said as she climbed back into the ute.

Taylah drove further down the driveway to the front gate. "How far can one little old lady over sixty run?"

Chapter Four

Jen sat forward in her seat, fear starting to gnaw at her stomach. Good question; how far had her aunt run? In a couple of hours it would get very chilly. "She's outsmarted us today. Let's park here and see if she's across the back road."

Jen ran down to the gate conscious of the fading light. She looked up at the half moon. Enough. She called out. "JoJo!" She waited. "You hear anything?" Taylah shook her head and together they walked down to the end of the driveway. Taylah held up a rusty letter box. "Look at this. It's been ripped off the post."

"What?" Jen ran over to her friend.

"Look", said Taylah, pointing to the post.

Jen looked about. Nobody came down the back road. It led to nowhere. She spotted something in the tall grass. "JoJo's done this, there's her hanky on the other side. It doesn't make any sense. She knows the postman doesn't deliver here. Why?"

Jen started to jog along the road; the movement helped stave off her growing anxiety. "Taylah, you look one side and I'll do the other."

As they progressed down the road, Jen listened out for movement or voices, but couldn't hear much above the sound of the local frogs, her own and Taylah's footsteps and the faint voices of her parents calling out for JoJo. She kept searching, her eyes scanning the last paddock of Whispering Mist and then the final paddock of Blue Orchard Park, Taylah's family property. They stopped at the top of the road.

With her hands on her hips Jen wandered out into the road, gulping in large lungful's of air. They were close at the crossroads. Which way now?

"Ssh! Did you hear that?" whispered Taylah.

Jen shook her head, and followed Taylah to the next block, further away from their properties.

Up ahead, they saw a figure walk out onto the road.

Jen's body trembled with relief as she realized it was her aunt. She waved her arms about and called, "JoJo, here we are."

Her aunt didn't respond. Jen sensed something was off.

She studied her aunt as best she could in the semi-darkness. *Strange.*

JoJo's cardigan had slid halfway down her back; in her hand she was swinging from side to side one of her fluffy dogs by the tail; her hair, which usually sat in a bun on top of her head, was loose. She looked bedraggled with her hair messed about her shoulders. All understandable in the circumstances, but something was odder than usual.

The girls jogged up to her. As they drew closer, JoJo turned and her face broke out into a smile - not one the girls were familiar with. Her face softened, a small lift of her eyebrows and a subtle change in her expression from alluring to seductive stunned them. This smile was not meant for them. She started to sway her body from side to side. They heard a soft high-pitched sound. A giggle?

Jen stalled, as did Taylah. "She's not seeing us," whispered Taylah.

Fear clutched at Jen's heart. *What's happened?*

As they drew up to her, JoJo's eyes darted between Taylah and Jen, and then she looked over their shoulders. JoJo's mouth fell open, and her eyes clouded with confusion.

"I'm sorry, JoJo, it's just us," whispered Jen, unsure how to handle this new side of her aunt.

JoJo stomped her feet like a child, turned, and ran further along the road, the way Jen and Taylah had come. She stopped at the crossroad and looked left and right.

Jen and Taylor followed. "JoJo, who are you waiting for?" Jen asked.

A whimper escaped JoJo's lips as she drew the soft toy up to her chest, and hugged it tight.

Jen reached out and gently laid a hand on her aunt's shoulder. JoJo shivered, her thin frame no match for the cool breeze coming down the valley. She tried again. "JoJo, who are you waiting for?" she repeated.

Taylah pulled JoJo's cardigan up and fussed about her hair, and all the while her aunt's jaw trembled as they shielded her from the cold.

Jen kissed the top of JoJo's head and put her arm in hers. "Let's go, JoJo; let's go home."

JoJo pulled at Jen's arms to keep her close. Her aunt glanced up at her with eyes now focused clear and steady. Jen's heart thudded in her chest at the rare event.

Disappointment flashed across her aunt's face.

Jen knelt beside her aunt and took her hand in hers. "JoJo, were you waiting for Uncle Stan?"

JoJo squeezed her eyes shut. "He promised," she whispered, with a raspy voice full of pain.

"Who?" asked Jen. Alert as never before. JoJo raised her arms and pushed her away, then she started powering on toward home.

What a nightmare.

Taylah followed JoJo.

Jen turned and did a slow three sixty. She loved this area and knew it so well. None of that helped her growing unease as she stared out into the bush around her. She'd always considered the bush her friend and loved its inhabitants. Jen saw the eyes that glowed from the bushes in the dead of night, heard their mating calls, and had rescued many.

Who was JoJo waiting for? Her senses were on high alert. Was someone out there watching them? What was so significant about today? First the graffiti on the car and now JoJo. Why?

Chapter Five

B rock Colder had no idea what he was doing when he walked into the Riverside Pub looking for his landlord, Reg Myles.

Scotch that.

He knew exactly what he was doing. For the first time in years he felt hope.

His mind had worked overtime all day mulling over Jen's ideas. At first he thought she was mad, talking the stuff of fairy dust, but on the drive back, after dropping her off this morning, he saw the rundown garage as something more. One thought led to another until all he could see were possibilities.

Dangerous thoughts for a man used to moving on.

Jen's words had breathed new life into him.

He braced himself not to get too carried away. For months, he'd spent so much time arguing with Gareth before finally planning this trip. After the month was up, that was it. Problem was, he hadn't given any thought to what came next in his life.

He knew he was mulling over a half-cocked idea, but it didn't deter him one bit. Brock had some vague idea old Reg might be in for a quick drink.

He couldn't see the bar for the wall-to-wall people surrounding it. After months of being on the road, the heat, noise and crowds slammed him hard.

Long weekend. Of course.

On a hunch he went over to the bar, waited his turn and bought two craft beers. He sidestepped people blocking paths, wait staff serving drinks and collecting empties, as he wound his way out of the bar area and headed toward the beer garden. He climbed down half a dozen steps and stood for a moment checking out each corner.

Sitting at a table on his own, going through the form guide, sat Reg Myles. Brock walked across to him.

"How you going, Reg?"

The old boy looked up, his glasses perched on the end of his nose, his thick snow white eyebrows matching the mop of hair that flopped about his neck and face.

A smile broke out across his worn tanned face. "Surprised to see you here."

Brock handed a beer to Reg and sat on the chair opposite. "Hope you like craft, they tell me this one's a good brew."

Reg raised an eyebrow as he lifted the cold glass of beer. "It's the right colour, right temperature. It'll go down well. Thank you."

Brock sat back and took a swig of the coloured brew. He never liked to rush a drink and after a solid day's work he welcomed the cold shot of beer. "Ah, that hit the spot."

The sudden laughter and loud cheers at a table nearby caught his attention. The noise stopped conversation at most tables, and heads turned. It was a family group celebrating as a waitress brought out a cake with a balloon attached, the words *Happy 60th Anniversary* visible. The *elderly* couple blushed at the attention, and after much noisy encouragement from their family, stood up and kissed each other.

The sound, deafening. Each table let out a wild cheer which descended into a lot of laughter in the room.

Brock smiled. He could not imagine knowing anybody for sixty years, let alone being married that long. Most of his relationships lasted around a year, but in his experience, that was when the turning point came, where he was put on notice and asked "Where is this leading?" He never had an answer to that question.

He took another sip. There had been two good women in his life that he should never have let go. He'd blamed it on his itinerant ways. Poor excuse; he just tagged along out of habit. First, with his father, because he was too young to do otherwise, and now with his brother. Then what? He doubted he had a single wanderlust cell in his body.

Reg folded away his guide and put aside his glasses. "I'm here every night and I haven't seen you boys in. Aren't you interested in a night off?"

Brock studied the drips of water sliding down his glass. "We're sorting ourselves out. And cleaning out your place has kept us busy."

Reg almost choked on his beer. "You hassled me for nigh on six months to get me to agree to open the place up. You knew what you were getting into."

Did he? It made him sick to his stomach when he thought of his agreement with his brother.

"I notice you've got some old beauties lined up," Brock said, referring to the cars lined up outside the shed. "What are your plans? You going to do them up?"

The old boy sat back. "I dreamt of working on them when I retired and then I kept putting retirement off and..."

"And?" prompted Brock.

Reg turned in his chair and faced him, a wave of sadness crossing his face. "Oh, boy, did I have some big dreams. I loved those dreams, saving hard for them, going without to get the money together and the excitement when those beautiful old cars rolled into the yard. I had big plans, but I made a fatal mistake." The old boy pursed his lips.

"What?"

"I kept my dreams on the shelf for too long. I'm now too old to reach them, the enthusiasm's gone and so has the interest. I still love those cars, but as for working on them, sourcing new engines, cleaning them up and everything else. Uh! I can't do it."

Brock heard, he understood, but he'd be dammed if he was going to let beautiful cars rot away to dust before his eyes.

"You're getting very philosophical there, Reg. I'm sure if you got started working on one, you'd get the bug again. I'm sure you could do it."

Reg shook his head. "Nah, I put my energy and heart into fixing everybody else's cars, and, as you can see, I haven't touched 'em in years. My own fault."

The two men sat silent for a bit, each with their own thoughts.

Brock stood up and raised his glass. "Reg, like another one? We need to talk some more."

By the time he'd returned to his chair and handed Reg a beer, his mind was made up.

He pushed aside his beer, and eyed the wily old mechanic. "Reg, how would you feel if I did up one of your cars? We could plan it together, but I'd do the work."

Reg sat up straighter, but kept his eyes on his beer.

Brock continued. "It's my line of work and I've gotta say, I love each and every one of those cars you've got out the back there. I can source the parts. It'd be a pleasure to work on."

Reg looked him in the eyes. "Why?"

Brock sat back and thought about that. It wasn't enough to say he loved the cars-so did Reg. "I can't walk past those beauties anymore and let them rot. Make no bones, Reg, they are in bad shape. Soon you'll sell them for a song and that's leaving them for someone else to fix. They might do an okay job, who knows? But, okay not what we want. We want them at their best and we both know what it's going to take to get them there."

Reg let out a deep sigh. "Which one first?"

"I love the 1930s Amal car you've got there. You could show her, she's quite something."

Reg frowned. "Show her?"

"Why not? Everybody loves history and old cars. We can source some parts, maybe in Europe, Italy, that's where you can get the right fit."

Reg studied him and Brock was buoyed by the twinkle in his eye. "You reckon you can find original parts in Europe? It'll cost."

Brock shrugged. "What doesn't? You want them restored properly, don't you?"

Brock controlled his own fears about the cost. His family always blamed a lack of money for holding back their lives, their dreams. It was his family's mantra. That's what had brought him and Gareth to Bindarra Creek.

Reg started to fiddle with his form guide, a frown forming.

Brock grinned at him. "I need you to work with me here, Reg. If not, nothing's going to happen. I know you don't know where this is going, or what it's going to cost, but…"

Reg cut in. "I'm part-way in", he growled. "I'll drop by tomorrow and we'll look at what needs to be done."

Brock could live with that. He reached out to shake Reg's hand. "Thanks, Reg. I appreciate it."

Reg cocked his head as they shook hands. "It's going to cost us."

Brock lifted his beer to his lips. "Cheers to that."

An hour later Brock strode out of the pub and pulled out his keys. He hummed to himself, pleased with how things were going. He hoped Reg would work with him. Even one or two days a week would be good, he was tired of working on his own.

At the end of the carpark, a movement caught his eye. A surge of anger shot through him. He stalked down to the end of the driveway and saw Gareth climb into his four-wheel drive.

Brock ran up and opened the vehicle door before Gareth had a chance to put his keys in the ignition. "If you've got something to say to me, say it, but don't go sneaking around spying on me."

Gareth glared at him. With both hands he grabbed the door and pulled hard to close it. He didn't succeed.

With a firm grip on the open door, Brock kept the distance between them. "Why didn't you come in for a drink? Why not show your face? Reg wouldn't have minded."

Gareth looked murderous and Brock knew his brother's anger knew no bounds.

His brother shifted in his seat and glanced about. "Keep your voice down. You know I want us to stay under the radar. You're built like the Hulk; once seen, never forgotten."

Brock almost laughed, but held back. He couldn't bear his brother's wrath. "I'm well aware of what you want. That's all I hear. I don't think having the odd beer or meal makes us stand out."

His brother smirked and in that moment Brock didn't care about playing Mr Nice Guy. "Now piss off."

Brock slammed the door shut and stalked back up the drive way. He heard Gareth start his engine; heard the low hum, the roar, and the sudden uptake signalling a gear change. The high-pitched scream of the souped-up engine followed by the ear-shattering screech of wheels caused Brock to turn around. Inside a blink, the vehicle shot up the short driveway and past him, its doors brushing the hairs on his arms.

His heart pounded in his chest.

Gareth stopped a couple of metres away. He wound down his window and yelled, "Don't you ever forget it's me in the driver's seat." Then he floored it, and the engine roared as Gareth drove out the carpark.

In seconds people were everywhere, rushing to him from the pub, from the car park out the back and the picnic area fronting the river. Stunned by the number of people showing up, Brock forced a 'thank you' smile and nodded to show he was okay.

Inside, he seethed.

When the last of his well-wishers walked away Brock headed straight for his suv.

Why hadn't he noticed it before? His brother was a real-life Dr Jekyll and Mr Hyde, unpredictable, ruthless and frightening.

He'd allowed himself to be part of this madness with Gareth. Why? He didn't care for the jewels or the money. Gareth was family and family meant home, didn't it? He shook his head, rattled by his thoughts. He could see it now. He yearned for something that no longer existed. With his father dead and his brother going down a frightening path, he had no family.

He needed to set his own path. First part, watch Gareth like a hawk over the next month. Second part? He wasn't sure, but he looked forward to Reg popping round and checking out his cars. Working on cars-that's what set his blood on fire.

Chapter Six

J en didn't know what to make of tonight's drama. Her family life worked like clock-work; rarely anything unusual happened to them. She waved goodbye to Taylah and now watched her mother usher a distressed JoJo inside. When the front door slammed shut Jen turned to her father.

Her father's ashen face matched the colour of the white-washed garage door behind him. He sat on a small plastic seat looking utterly lost. Jen's heart ached for him. Despite all their years of caring for JoJo, she'd never seen either of her parents so distressed. Their lives were difficult with JoJo, but from what she could tell, they were coping.

Tonight she could see the toll caring for JoJo was having on her parents. The one recurring question - how long could they continue to care for her – was never spoken aloud. Never, ever.

"Dad, do you want to go inside for a cuppa? Get comfortable?"

He shook his head. "No, I'll wait out here for a bit." He gave her a wry smile. "I'll wait until JoJo's in bed."

Jen stepped down the stairs and sat on the ground beside him. They were protected from the breeze and it wasn't often she had her father to herself. She wrapped her arm around her father's lower leg and laid her head against his thigh. "What do you make of this?"

"No idea. JoJo's never run off before."

"She was waiting for someone, Dad. I'm sure of it. She didn't recognise Taylah and me. For a moment I think she thought we were someone else."

Her father let out gruff laugh. "Perhaps it was Stan. They were only married for a year when he died."

"What about the jewels? Could this have anything to do with the graffiti?"

Her words hung in the air between them.

After a while, her father patted her head. "It's ancient history now, but well before you were born. JoJo and Stan opened a small jewellery shop in town a few months after they married. Anyway about a year later they were robbed."

Jen pulled away from her father so she could see his face. "What was taken?"

"They were cleaned out. All the trays of jewellery and cash, even in the safe. I think a few pieces were left behind, but they forced JoJo to empty each tray into some bags. It wasn't a lot back then. Bindarra Creek didn't have the numbers to support a large jewellery shop."

"What did they sell?"

"Oh, the usual, engagement rings, wedding rings and a few rings for twenty-firsts and the odd egg cups and baby things for christenings."

Jen stood up, grabbed her father's hand and pulled him up with her. "Come on, it's getting late."

Without hesitation he returned his chair to the garage and closed the door. She linked arms with him and together they walked to the homestead. "So, why would someone come here searching for the jewels?"

Her father stopped, his expression thoughtful. "Maybe it's not only the jewels they're after. JoJo also emptied the till and the safe. It all went into a satchel. I don't know-just like I don't know why the robbers came here after the robbery, and didn't head straight for Sydney."

Stunned, JoJo stared at her father. "They came back here? Are you sure?"

Her father nodded as he opened the front door and ushered her inside. "Their car was seen driving back here. None of it makes sense. All three robbers were signed up to join the army and were due to start their training a week after the robbery."

Jen bit the inside of her cheek, her mind churning over this latest revelation. Why had her parents never spoken of this before now? Why? Why? Why?

Her mother padded down the hallway. "You pair were out there long enough," chided her mother. "Let's get to bed; I'm bushed."

Jen leaned against the front door. "What do you reckon, Dad? Why us? Why now?"

Her father gave her a quick peck on the cheek. "No idea. Get to bed, you've got a big day tomorrow."

She followed her parents down the hall and leaned against their bedroom door frame.

"Why would they come back here other than to divvy up the jewels? Was there a fight? What happened?"

There was a joint gasp from her parents. Her father pulled out his pyjamas from under the pillow and her mother drew the blinds.

Her mother pulled a face. "Let it go, Jen. No jewels were ever found. The shearers here at the time did not mention any fight. That Friday they finished up early and all the guys headed off to the nearest pub. Other than that I can't answer you."

Agitated, Jen stepped into the room. "Some of those shearers had to be lying. Are you sure they didn't leave the jewels here? What about the money? Has anything ever been found?"

He shook his head. "Oh, Jen, this is such a nonsense. Do as your mother says, let it go. Neither the jewels nor the money were ever found."

"What, none of them?"

He pulled off his boots. "Don't you think if I'd found them we'd be living a little better?"

His pained expression cut deep. It stymied any comforting words. She'd do almost anything to see ease her parents' gruelling life.

Maybe as the years rolled on, they'd grown used to the financial struggle. Jen had seen the worst, when they were forced to sell a couple of acres to the McKenna's. Her parents' lives were hard. As a jockey her father could only do the country circuit and he averaged five to seven rides a week. Lately, the fee for one ride only covered the petrol cost of the roundtrip to the track.

She let out a frustrated sigh. "Okay, where have you searched?"

Her father raised his arm. "It's a case of where haven't I searched. I've dug up around the trees near the sheds, around the old shearing shed and even dug up the foundations to the garden shed. Not a jewel or satchel to be found. I reckon someone's got them, or they're well hidden somewhere."

"Really?"

He tossed her a pillow which she managed to catch. "Could be the McKenna's are sitting on a little gold mine. Now get out of here."

***

Hours later Jen lay wide awake in her bed. Each time she answered one of her questions; more questions arose, and like mushrooms they multiplied in the dark. Agitated, she turned and faced her clock radio. It was just past two am. In a couple of hours her father would be up and about getting ready to do some track work with Hannah McKenna next door. Hannah's schedule was punishing and she was determined to be the most successful thoroughbred horse trainer in the district. Jen curled her body, and snuggled up against her blankets and pillow in an effort to relax and sleep.

Five minutes later, in frustration she climbed out of bed and headed for the kitchen. In the pantry she couldn't find any cake or biscuits. Damn. She swung across to the fridge and pulled out the vanilla yoghurt, a half-tub full of strawberry ice cream, a punnet each of berries and cut-up pieces of strawberries. She tossed the berries and yoghurt into the ice cream tub and then sprinkled some crushed almonds on top.

Perfect.

Clutching the bowl of ice-cold goodies, she managed to open the sliding door to the verandah. She walked around to the side of the property that overlooked the valley where their empty paddocks, once full of sheep, then horses blended, with the McKenna's.

She walked past Molly and Sam, their two golden retrievers. They looked sleepy. Sam climbed out of their bed to join her. Molly struggled to climb out with her arthritic joints. Jen patted them both, urging Sam to stay in bed. After a minute he nestled in beside Molly once more.

Jen couldn't wait to lie along the well-worn lounge, having kicked the pillows to the side arm which faced the valley. She sank into the cushions and sank her spoon into the cold mush. After a couple of deep breaths of the cool fragrant air, Jen waited.

Useless.

Normally just being out on the verandah, alone, in the dead of night calmed her jagged nerves. Not tonight. She dug her spoon deep into the mix and again sucked on the cool goo. After another two spoonful's, Jen gave up and lay the bowl down on the floor.

What is it with me tonight?

Annoyed with herself, she got up and paced the length of the verandah.

Jen strolled to the other end of the verandah and wondered how much the police would reveal. She hoped they did not put up the privacy wall.

The screen door slid open. "Oh, Jen," whispered her mother. "What are you doing out here?"

Jen shrugged. "I couldn't sleep."

Her mother's eyes took in the now melted goo. "None of us can tonight. I think you should get to bed, and try to get some sleep. You've got a big day tomorrow."

"Mum, why did you never mention how Uncle Stan died? All I knew is that he died young-from a heart attack, I thought."

Her mother took one step out onto the verandah. As if sensing her scrutiny, her mother met her gaze head on. "He did, that's exactly what killed him. Now come on, get to bed." Without another word her mother swung around and went inside.

Jen leaned against the back wall and stared out into the darkness. She usually cherished this quiet time on her own in the darkness, but tonight all that had changed. Somehow the spell had been broken. Her mother wasn't to blame. Jen could no longer tolerate the chaos and noise of JoJo. It wore her out. So did the idea of leaving her parents alone to deal with JoJo.

At twenty-four years it was high time she "*set herself on fire*". Her first call would be to ask Laurie to make her job permanent, then borrow some money and buy a place of her own. How hard could that be?

Energised, she picked up the bowl of goo, went inside and dumped it in the sink.

Chapter Seven

"The printer's not working, again. Could some-body please put a call in to that whiz kid who sold it? How many calls does it take?" Laurie's voice roared down the hallway.

Mel grimaced. "It's Sunday, Laurie. He won't come out today. I've left messages."

"Leave it with me, Laurie," said Jen. "I'll check it." She ran down to the small stationary room, where the printer sat against the back wall. Jen leaned across the bench and switched on the power. The printer kicked into gear and spat out twenty copies of the latest statistics about Bindarra Creek.

Jen collated them and handed the small booklets to Laurie. She grinned at him. "I've got the magic touch today. Here you go."

Laurie sat back. "That's great, thanks, Jen."

She hung around the door. "Laurie, will you have a spare five minutes today?"

His dark eyes shot her a knowing look. "What's this about?"

Her nerves almost stopped her. *Heavens, Jen, you're not asking him to cut off his arm.*

She straightened her jacket. "I wanted to discuss how I'm going and whether you'd consider making me permanent. I know we haven't had the discussion yet."

Laurie paused a moment, then slid the booklets into a folder. "No, we haven't. Let me give it some thought and I'll get back to you. Today's not a good day."

Jen backed away. "Sure, Laurie. That's okay. I can wait."

Like a scalded cat, she fled down the corridor to the safety of her desk. She popped a jelly bean in her mouth, glad the worst part of the day was over. Was that progress? She wasn't too sure, but at least she'd started the conversation.

"Jen," called out Laurie. "We've got someone interested in the unit upstairs. He's coming this morning. Would you mind checking it out? Take the dustpan and brush and get rid of any dead cockroaches."

She jumped up, excited to finally get to see the top floor-unit. "Of course, onto it now."

With the dustpan and brush in hand Jen climbed the four sets of stairs until she reached the top floor. Laurie had purchased the building over three years ago and had spent a minor fortune updating it. He'd managed to lease the two-bedroom unit directly above the agency, but for months he'd had no takers to either buy or rent the top-floor one-bedroom unit.

She opened the door and walked in. *Wow*. She stood in awe of the wall-to-wall white – white walls, white floors, white ceilings, and the palest grey granite bench in the kitchen.

Jen soaked up the cool vibe of the small, but compact space. She breathed in the silence, and loved that she couldn't hear a thing from outside. The silence was like a soothing balm. She relished the lush feel of all white, and the privacy.

She ran across to the front window and looked out. Main Street was busy for a Monday morning with people heading to The Cyprus Café for breakfast and others cruising down the street … silent.

Jen marvelled at the kitchen. With a small dishwasher, a narrow pantry with plenty of shelving, and a huge and long window at the sink, overlooking the carpark, it was fantastic. The large bedroom surprised her and there was a lovely reading nook by the bay window overlooking Main Street. She could live here. *This is wonderful.*

The door swung open.

Mel joined her. "What do you think? You can see why this is still on the market, can't you? It's the runt of the pack. It's the only one-bedroom in town. Why my back porch is bigger than this whole place. Yours too, Jen. Not many calls for one-bedders."

Jen gripped the dust pan. "I think it's lovely."

Mel scoffed. "You need to get out more. This place lacks personality."

Jen walked across to the window overlooking Main Street. "It's a solid build. The wind's picked up outside and not a window rattles."

Mel looked at her in horror. "Don't tell me that. We'd better call in those painters, they've probably painted over the window sills and now they're stuck." Mel's phone buzzed. "The potential is here. I'll send him up and you can show him around. Let me know if the windows are stuck."

"Okay. What's Laurie going to do? Sell it, or lease it?"

"Sell," called out Mel as she raced down the stairs.

Jen ran around the unit searching for dead cockroaches, but couldn't find any, and had just reached the kitchen sink when the door opened.

"Anybody in?"

The deep melodious voice echoed in the unit and caught her off guard. Jen froze as Brock strode into the room. The other day he'd looked hot, but today - dressed in blue jeans, a dark blue shirt and his blond hair still damp from a shower - he looked hotter than hades.

When he spotted her, his face broke out into a warm smile. "Hi, Jen."

Jen took in a deep breath, "Hi." Her face almost burst trying to suppress an enthusiastic smile, but she held fast onto a more professional expression. Still, she could feel her face blush and she had nowhere to hide. She prayed she didn't make a fool of herself, and then she did.

She raised her arms to show the dustpan and brush. "Sorry, you caught me out - I was looking for dead cockroaches and didn't find any. I'll just put these away."

In seconds the dustpan and brush disappeared in the cupboard under the sink.

He walked into the room and her rehearsed spiel fell away. "I didn't think you'd be interested in a one-bedder."

Brock grinned at her. "Why not? It might be in my price bracket. Anyway I'm just gathering info."

"I see." Jen walked over to the front window. "What you see is what you get. The largest room in the place is the bedroom, and we're not even sure if the windows open."

In half a dozen steps Brock strode across to the front window, turned the lock and pushed. The window flew up.

He faced her, a knowing glint in his eye. "They work. Anything else wrong with the place? It looks pretty good to me."

She pulled a face. "This unit is a sandwich - one side you've got the traffic noise from Main Street and right opposite you've got the carpark outside. Cars are in and out all day. If you're after peace and quiet, well, you've lucked out here."

Jen studied him as he walked about inspecting the kitchen. He dwarfed the place.

He grinned at her, a twinkle in his eye. "Jennifer Rogers, do you have someone else interested in this place? I swear you're trying to talk me out of it."

She blushed. Embarrassed, she did an about turn and busied herself opening the bathroom door. So what if she liked the way he said her name?

He blocked her re-entry to the lounge room with his body. Startled, she was shocked at his closeness. She caught his ginger spicy scent and all kinds of delicious and inappropriate thoughts devoured her brain. Not a good thing to happen at a showing.

Brock's lips curved into a smile. "You are. Who are you saving it for? Yourself? I would if I were you. It's a good place in a great location."

She ducked under his arm. "It's out of my reach. Now, back onto you. I hear you've got a short-term lease of six months at Reg's place. Are you passing through or sticking around?"

Her words hung in the air. They'd flown out without passing quality control in her brain. They were out and she couldn't do much about it now. She held her breath, and waited.

He scrunched his face. "Haven't yet decided. It depends on a few things."

Laurie's friendly "meet and greet" voice floated up to them. Trust Laurie's hot air to rise and invade this beautiful space.

"Are you part of Laurie's Q&A this morning?"

He nodded.

Jen collected the dustpan and brush from the cupboard. "Okay, it sounds as though it's started. He wouldn't want you to miss it. It should be interesting."

Brock gave her a thoughtful look. "Jen, I've brought my bike into town. Would you be interested in going for a ride and showing me about later this afternoon?"

She stared at him, thrilled that he'd asked her, and fought a strong urge to say yes.

He would be hers for a few hours. She liked that idea. How tempting was that?

But, she'd want more. Jen realised she was seriously attracted to Brock, and she was done with the ones who passed through. She'd wasted too many months, and they added up to years, with guys who might stick around, and then headed for the big smoke.

He leaned closer. "Well?"

His voice made her quiver; he touched a nerve every time he used that deep tone.

By the time Jen found her voice, Brock had moved closer to her. "Sorry, Brock. I'm not free today."

His handsome face shut down. He nodded, and then slowly walked away from her and made his way to the door. "Okay, I understand. Catch you later."

She doubted he did understand.

Jen heard him climb down the stairs and she cursed herself. It would be so easy to go out with him, but in her heart, she knew it would become a memory, a keepsake for the future. it wouldn't serve any purpose other than to colour her future with someone else.

Chapter Eight

The sound of the doorbell reverberated loudly throughout the empty offices. Jen's phone buzzed and she read Taylah's text: *Are you in? Is this where you're spending Sunday night?*

Jen opened the office's front door to Taylah. "Bloody Laurie, he's got me working tonight."

Her friend let out a laugh. "I had a hunch you were here when I saw the light on. What's he got you doing?"

Jen waved her arm toward the five opened boxes of brochures on the floor. "He's wearing me out, I swear. He wants all of these brochures folded and put in envelopes with his business card so he can hand them out tomorrow."

Taylah rolled her eyes.

"Exactly. We didn't manage to do it today. We were packed with people coming in wanting his business his card and a list of properties, and we ran out of brochures. You can imagine how well that went down. The printer hasn't stopped all afternoon."

Taylah picked up the closest box and sat at Mel's desk. "So, today went well for him?"

Jen nodded. "Yes, he must be crowing. More people turned up for his Q&A's than had booked. He had a third impromptu one during lunch. People are really interested in Bindarra Creek-it stunned us."

Taylah rolled up her sleeves. "Okay, let's finish this."

Hours later Jen sat back in her chair. Her jelly bean bowl stood empty, they were out of milk and both girls were hungry. "Enough. I vote we head for the Riverside for a quick meal. Mel and I can finish this up tomorrow morning. There's only half a box to go."

Taylah pushed back her box of envelopes. "I second that."

"Good." Jen scooted up the last of the envelopes and ran down to the kitchen to tidy things up.

Her phone buzzed and she read her mother's text: *When do you think you'll be home?*

Jen texted: *Taylah's finishing it with me and then we're going to the Riverside to eat. Home around ten.* She paused before she hit the send button.

The image of her mother's sad expression when they'd brought JoJo home sprang into Jen's mind. It had shocked her to the core to see her strong, capable mother so sad. She should go home and help her.

JoJo, like a second shadow, rarely left her mother's side, but Jen realized now that her mother hid behind her mantra of "if you have to take on an unpleasant job you should always do it in good cheer". Her mother had done that and more for decades. When would she call it a day?

Could she rope in her father as an ally to tell her mother that it was time to think about organising some respite care for JoJo to give her mother a break. Would her mother listen?

She smiled at her own suggestion. They had to start the conversation sometime. Taylah's mother had once broached the subject of moving JoJo to a nursing home, but Jen's mother flatly refused. Maybe the time had come to discuss it because after recent events her parents needed some sort of circuit breaker, and soon.

"Hey," called out Taylah. "Take a look at this. What do you reckon is going on out there?"

Jen joined Taylah at the front office window by Mel's desk. Her best friend stood staring through the slashes of the blind checking out Main Street.

Taylah grinned at her. "Check this out. These guys are walking in every direction from the cenotaph. I've been watching them for a while now."

"What?"

Curious, Jen slowly pulled back the venetian blind.

In the soft glow of the street light Jen studied the two dark figures as they stood in front of the cenotaph facing the street. In unison they looked up in the direction of the girls, but their gaze settled on something much further along. Jen's chest tightened as she recognized the familiar figures.

Surprise and disappointment shunted through her at seeing Brock pointing to several buildings down the street. What they were doing? Walking in several different paths from the cenotaph? Why? It looked like a normal thing to do, but her gut did not agree.

Her eyes zeroed in on Gareth Colder. In his hand he held a tight grip on a leash to a fully grown German Shepherd. She knew it. That threatening bark she'd heard did not belong to a pup.

There was something edgy about Gareth that he needed to walk the streets at night with a dog, maybe even a lethal weapon for all she knew. She knew a few of her parents' friends had German Shepherds as guard dogs. They could be friendly, but could turn quickly as when they needed to.

She dropped her hold on the blind and leaned against the wall. Her body prickled hot and cold. "Unbelievable. It's the Colder brothers. The ones I met yesterday morning at Reg's garage. What on earth are they doing?"

Taylah reached out and spread two slats of the blind and peered out. "Really? They're counting steps looking for something."

Jen frowned. "Counting steps?"

Taylah leaned closer to the window. "Look, they're starting again in another direction. They stop when they reach a certain number. This is their third round."

"Damn," muttered Taylah. " Now they're out of sight."

"What?"

Taylah pulled up the blind. "Take a look. It's a full moon. You can just make out their long shadows. They've stopped and I think they're right on that far corner where Hamilton's the butchers were. What do you reckon?"

Jen stood on her toes and studied the shadows. Taylah was right. In a blink the shadows disappeared.

She grabbed her friend's arm, as an unexpected mix of excitement and trepidation rippled throughout her body. "Brock came in this morning looking at Laurie's one-bedder. They might be just out for a walk, checking the town out. I have no idea. Come on, let's count steps."

Jen checked the office looked semi-tidy before she locked the front door. Outside the cool night air settled over them and they zipped up their jackets.

Jen rubbed her hands together. "Now, let's work this out. I can't believe we're doing this. We're standing in Main Street and nobody is about on a Sunday night."

Taylah let out a nervous laugh. "I bet they're in the shadows watching us."

Jen ran across to the cenotaph. "You've read too much into things. I don't care if they are. What does it matter?"

She pulled back her wind-blown hair, unsure of just why doing this excited her. She and Taylah clearly needed to get out more-more than a week in Sydney, perhaps an overseas holiday?

She hugged her jacket about her. "What do you reckon? Which direction first?"

Taylah looked about. "I think you'd better do the walking and I'll count. You've got longer legs than me and their strides looked to be about a metre long. Okay?"

Jen nodded.

"As for direction, I think the last one worked for them. They haven't come here to try again."

Jen dug her hands into her pocket. "I'm ready when you are."

Taylah hesitated, looking about. "You think they've gone? I mean they could be lurking anywhere."

"Oh, come on, Taylah," moaned Jen. "They have that huge German Shepherd with them. Don't you think it would bark? They're not all obedient."

Taylah didn't look too convinced. "Okay, start in the direction of Hamilton's."

Jen stepped out.

As they approached the old butchery she glanced across at her friend. Taylah's arm swung in the air at each step, keeping count. Not even the odd call from the bats above messed with Taylah's concentration.

When they reached the junction Taylah held up her arm. "Stop."

"Are you sure?" Jen's breath almost caught in her throat.

Taylah turned toward her, her face grim. "It's close enough and you're not going to like it. At this spot here." She marked an imaginary line in the street. "It hits one hundred and fifty metres. You know where that is, don't you?"

Stunned, Jen stared at her friend.

The old wooden post, the very one from which JoJo had ripped off the letter box, was marked one hundred and fifty, the address of the old homestead.

Taylah shivered, and glanced left and right down the street. "You really think they've gone? I don't remember hearing a car, or a motorbike."

Jen stared up at the sky for a few seconds before she shifted her glance to Taylah. Perplexed, she ran a hand through her hair. *Why the old address? What's significant about that? It isn't used today.*

Then they heard it. A dog's threatening growl, low, deep and close-by.

Chapter Nine

Brock Colder clenched his fists as he watched his brother rein in T-Rex. Why, Why frighten the girls? Why issue them with a warning? Why let them know they're being watched?

"Why?" he hissed.

Gareth gave him a satisfied smirk. "For fun. I couldn't resist."

Brock turned away in disgust, but not for long. He studied the young women as they ran into the shadows of the shops opposite. All he could see were darker movements in the shadows. He heard their light steps echo down the street and then stop, followed by the slam of a door. He stepped past his brother hoping to see something, a light, anything as he stared down Main Street.

Where the hell had they come from? What were they doing in town at this hour? How long had they been watching them count bloody steps? How much did they see? Did Jen suspect it was them?

He shut his eyes in the hope of stopping the endless questions.

When would he learn? His brother roped him in every time. Now he'd be in for a sleepless night because the questions were endless.

Their father, as usual, had led them down a sad track. His vague story from his past about stolen jewels and money being hidden on a property had filled his brother with hope. After months of pressure from Gareth he'd caved in and agreed to search for them. He should have known better. Caving into his brother's wishes always got him in trouble.

When would he learn?

Brock walked out into the centre of Main Street and spied the real estate business. The girls were there, he knew it in his gut. In Tamworth it had sounded so easy to find a hidden treasure underneath the cement floor of a disused shearing shed on a property miles out of town. His father's last words - *"only a couple of paddocks away from the main house"* - had set his brother off to find this hidden treasure.

With intensity he stared at the Laurie's office for any movement inside. In their haste neither he nor Gareth had given any thought to the people connected with that treasure.

Gareth slapped him on the arm. "Come on, let's go."

Brock stood firm, his gaze still on Laurie's office. "You didn't have to do that. There was no need to scare the girls."

His brother stood behind him and swung his arm about Brock's neck, into a head-lock. "T-Rex did his job. T-Rex and Jasper are the perfect pair, like us. Everybody runs to Jasper and falls in love, but it's T-Rex that keeps everyone in line. Like us. It's why others like us, love us."

Brock raised his hands and prised off his brother's hold about his neck. In one quick movement he shoved his brother against the nearest wall where only minutes earlier they'd stood hiding. "What do you mean 'others like us'?"

His brother's unhinged high-pitched laugh chilled him. He glared at his brother. When had his brother, the smart, educated one, changed? Or, had he chosen to put Gareth in the too hard box and ignored his growing dominance?

"The boys in Tamworth, they loved working with us, they trusted us."

Gareth stood an inch away, his hot breath streaming across Brock's face, then broke away from him. "Yes, us. I'm talking about the gang. If you haven't noticed, to the gang we're rough and ready. You're the rough one, the muscle man they trust, and I'm the ready one, the cool brains behind the scenes, plotting our next move. Like I'm doing now and this town will know it soon. We'll make a mark here. We might be brawn and brains, but I like rough and ready, that's us. It works, bro."

Gareth's eyes flashed bright, with a zeal Brock had not seen before.

"We're close to this, I can feel it. It's unreal. The ideas keep popping up in my brain. I thought we'd sneak up here after dinner and check things out and look who we find sneaking about?"

Brock willed himself to stay calm. From bitter experience he knew it wasn't worth fighting his brother. Gareth's meanness and nastiness knew no bounds and he could see his plans causing some serious damage involving the police. As strangers they stood out. At the garage they were sitting ducks.

All the arrows were pointed downwards if this latest escapade did not end well.

Maybe it was time to move on. They'd been itinerant all their lives, they knew the drill.

It meant leaving friends behind, changing schools, keeping people at arm's length and keeping to yourself.

But now he'd met Jen, and he wanted to stay for once. He could see her mind ticking over this morning. He knew she was interested in him, and he liked that she was. But she'd pushed back against his invitation to spend time with him. He'd love to be a fly on the wall in her brain and find out why.

Tamworth had changed everything. Their father's cancer meant they stayed longer than usual, and Gareth had joined the local bikie group. Those boys welcomed him with open arms.

T-Rex growled, pulling Brock back into the present. Gareth and T-Rex were walking toward their four-wheel drive. Mid-way Gareth stopped, lifted his head to the sky and let out a long loud howl. T-Rex followed with his own howl. Gareth let out another two long howls.

A shot of hot acid burned deep in Brock's stomach. He'd promised to see this out. He'd promised his father and promised his brother. Brock rubbed his stomach.

He raced across to his brother. "Shut up. What is going on with you?"

Gareth smiled at him. "It's okay, bro. I'm just happy. Happy with the way things are going and I just had to let it out."

Please god let's find these jewels or the money soon. He didn't care which it was. He'd often said he'd do anything to be free of his brother's madness. He promised himself this would be the last time. The very last time.

He straightened his back and pulled out his keys. Brock climbed into the suv and waited until his brother had settled T-Rex down in the back seat.

His attention shifted to a small hatchback pulling out from a carpark about half a dozen shops down. As the car stopped before driving onto the road, Brock saw a blonde head look left and right, checking for traffic, before driving onto the road.

He smiled to himself. He wanted to reassure her she was fine, the streets were clear. No matter what, deep in her bones Jennifer Rogers would always be on the straight and narrow, and do the right thing.

Chapter Ten

Agitated, Jen was glad they were headed home. She felt spooked.

"I'm going to start a 'list' of incidents and hand it over to the police. Things are piling up," Jen stated. She couldn't wait for this long weekend to be over.

Taylah switched on her high beams as they turned off the main road. "Do you want me to start early on those envelopes with you before Laurie turns up tomorrow? I'm up early."

Jen shook her head. "Thanks mate, but you're not working for Laurie. You've done enough. Look at what time it is! I can't wait to get to bed. I'm so tired."

Physically yes, mentally no. Her mind was hot-wired. Something was going on and she didn't know what. She sensed something was hanging over their heads.

Taylah turned right, and the car lights shone on the words *Whispering Mist* on the tired-looking sign which hung on the gate to her family's property.

She gathered her things as Taylah drove up to the homestead.

Her best friend looked bushed. Taylah rarely said no to her and tomorrow morning she and Jen's father would ride track work for Hannah, who was starting to make a name for herself as a horse trainer. The four am starts didn't stop for anything.

As they approached the homestead Jen saw the light on in her father's garage. She let out a sigh. What now? It was well past her father's bedtime.

Taylah drove the car up as close to the garage as possible. "Have you asked JoJo?"

Jen shook her head. "I did think of asking her, but she gets worked up and everybody pussy foots around her. It's worth a shot, though."

Taylah nodded toward the garage. "Check your dad's inside first. I'll wait just in case.'

Jen climbed out. "Okay. Have a good one."

She wrapped her jacket tight and started to shiver as the cool night air swirled about her. She closed the door and started down the pebbled pathway to the shed. Her feet crunched against the small stones when she heard the faint cries of JoJo followed by her mother's voice coming from the house.

Jen stopped mid-stride, torn between seeing her father or going inside to help her mother with JoJo. Her aunt's nightmares were getting worse as she grew older.

She waited a moment more, the anguished cries stopped, and with a heavy heart Jen headed down the path to her father.

Enough. Something had to be done. Her parents had skirted around the issue of looking into respite care for JoJo. Her mother did the lion's share of caring and needed a break. Jen used to spend much more time with JoJo, but Laurie kept her busy most evenings calling potential clients about properties they'd viewed the prior weekend.

When she reached the open door she popped her head in and spied her father sitting on an old camp chair surrounded by cards.

Jen turned and gave Taylah the thumbs-up. Taylah nodded and backed out of the driveway.

Jen stepped inside the doorway. Her father's passion for horses lived inside this shed. The walls were lined with saddles, straps and whips. At the far wall were photos of her father on various horses; some were his favourites and others were winners. He loved them all.

In the silence, Jen stood a while and studied her father.

Her heart clenched at his thinning grey hair-she doubted he yet knew about the growing bald patch at the back of his head - at the deep lines etched across his forehead, at his loose jowls, and at his hands, those tender, thoughtful hands that controlled a horse in full flight and comforted a sick animal with the slightest and most tender touch, now thick and scarred.

She set her bags down on the nearest bench, the noise echoing in the aluminium shed, but he didn't move. Puzzled, she walked over to him as he sifted through what looked like a box of cards.

Not wanting to startle him, she whispered, "Dad, what are you doing?"

He looked up, his eyes wide with surprise. A warm smile burst across his face. "Hello, pet. Good day?"

"Not one of my better ones. Laurie's kept us busy with his Q&A's and I'm waiting to get the car back," she said as she searched around and found the mate to her father's camp chair. Jen opened it and sat beside him.

She peered into the box on his lap. "That's my day in a nutshell. What've have you got there?"

When her father didn't answer, she grabbed the box and started sifting through them.

"Dad, all these cards have a yellow rose on the front and inside they all say *'til next time'*."

Her father nodded. "They're addressed to JoJo. Every year someone has been sending her these cards on the anniversary of the robbery. To make matters worse they use the old homestead address. She checks that letterbox every year."

"Really?" That silly, useless word shot out of her mouth before the ramifications of her father's quietly spoken words nestled into her brain. Jen's blood iced over. Brock and Gareth were walking one hundred and fifty steps.

Their old homestead's property number one hundred and fifty. Was there a connection?

She slumped in the chair. "As some kind of sick joke?"

Her father shook his head, his sad eyes glistening with tears. "This has gone on for too long and we just want it to end."

Jen took the small box of cards from her father's lap and checked them out. The same message on each. "Any idea who?"

Her father shifted in his seat. "We can only think it's from one of the guys at the time who robbed the store, or who worked as a shearer at the time and is annoyed he missed his cut and this is his little joke."

"What set JoJo off yesterday?"

"There wasn't a letter yesterday. And then this came in the mail for her. It was left in our letterbox. See? No postage."

He pulled out a card from his shirt pocket and handed it to her. "Similar card with a yellow rose on the front. Read inside."

Jen took the card and opened it. *See you at the crossroads.* She sat back in the chair, stunned that she didn't know about this latest piece of information. Are Brock and Gareth connected? They were pacing out one hundred and fifty steps. Would Gareth or Brock know about the anniversary card? How would they know? Alan Colt? Colder? Maybe she's looking for things to line up. Maybe she's got it all wrong.

"We've tried to shield you, pet. You need to concentrate on your job, but today your mother's tried everything to calm JoJo down. She's cooked her favourite meal, taken her for a drive and played shop. Your mother's exhausted."

Jen laid her hands over her father's callused hands as they sat in his lap. "Don't say another word. This has to stop."

Her father drew in a deep breath, his voice quivering. "JoJo's mind started to go just after the robbery. It's much worse now and we're all getting older."

Jen had only ever known JoJo in her current childlike state. She studied her father's quivering jaw. It was time to step up. "Dad, she needs to be properly assessed and from there we can make decisions. We don't know what that means, but it's not fair on any of us."

It felt good to finally say the words that for too many years had lain trapped and unspoken. Sounding firm to her father did not come naturally, but if she didn't take the reins, who would? Things were crystal clear. Both her parents were too heavily invested in JoJo's care to imagine another way of doing things.

He nodded. "You'd better tell your mum, then. I've tried, and she resists any change for JoJo."

Chapter Eleven

At five am the next morning Jen drove to the old mechanic's workshop. After a sleepless night her head ached. Thankfully her parents hadn't asked too many questions about her early start. From the Kingfisher Bridge she spied the old garage and couldn't see anyone about.

The fiery words she'd shot across to both Gareth and Brock in her head during her restless night were now being engulfed in fear and apprehension. Her resolve to tackle them about last night were starting to crumble.

She parked her car near the top of their driveway and climbed out. The cool morning air whipped about her.

A dog growled. She couldn't see him, but she wasn't about to hop into its pen.

Jen walked across to the driveway and waited. No way was she stepping onto their property.

The side door to the garage flew open and Brock poked his head out the door. His eyes widened in surprise when he saw her. Jen's rigid body relaxed a little.

"I'll put some shoes on. Give me a minute."

Jen's nerves kicked into gear and she started to pace. Her planned opening lines were a distant memory. In a couple of minutes later Brock walked toward her, a querulous expression on his face.

He rubbed his hands against the cold. "Morning, Jen. What's up?"

Jen slid her hands into the pockets of her trousers in an effort to cut out her emotion. She did not want her hands waving about explaining things as her anxiety grew. His casual easy manner almost disarmed her.

At such close proximity Brock's masculinity over-whelmed her. She took a step back. "I saw you and Gareth last night and I know you saw Taylah and me. I know what one hundred and fifty means. Do you? Is your father Alan Colt? But, he's now Alan Colder?"

Damn. Jen silently cursed herself. She'd spilled the lot to him in one go.

She waited.

Brock rocked back and forth, his eyes never leaving her face. His casual attitude infuriated her. She'd just landed some pretty heavy evidence against him. "I'm glad we've cleared the air."

Whoosh. So he knows! She let out a sigh. "Agreed. So, how did you find us?" She spat her words out like bullets.

Brock walked across to her hatch-back and leaned against it. "Dad gave us the old address and your surname. You were easy to find. Dad died a couple of months ago and told us about the robbery and that the loot hadn't been found."

Jen let that sink in. She struggled to cope with his easy-going manner.

"Why damage Laurie's car?" Jen asked.

Brock scrunched his face. "I'm sorry about that. Gareth plays games and that was one of them. I didn't think he'd do it, but he did. What can I say?"

Jen rubbed her forehead. Brock had been so upfront and all his explanations were plausible and probably true. Could she believe him? He and Gareth shared the same blood, history and everything else. Part of her so wanted to believe him, but he could have pulled out at any time. He's supporting his brother. He's tainted.

Brock frowned. "What are you doing here, Jen?"

She swallowed hard. What a shame he's passing through.

"I'm here to put you on notice. I know what you're after and there are no jewels. If there were we'd be living differently."

"Are you sure about that?" Brock asked.

Jen walked past him and opened the car door. She'd said her piece and would leave it at that. She'd take her notes to the police.

Brock pushed himself off the car. "Jen, hold up for a bit. After the robbery, the guys returned to the property to divvy up. It was a mad scramble and my father walked away empty handed. Something went wrong. Either somebody took the loot from them, or they hid it. Simple as."

Frustrated, she hadn't made her point strong enough she stepped closer to him. "You can stop. There's nothing to find. My father has dug up everywhere searching for them."

Brock looked her straight in the eye. His blue eyes were so close she noticed small darker coloured flecks. "Are you sure about that?"

Jen bristled. "What are you suggesting?"

"I'm being rational and looking at every possibility."

Jen didn't answer. She walked away, slid into her car and started the engine.

Brock knocked on her window and she wound it down. "What?" she asked.

He shook his head. "Something went down that day, but the jewels never left the property. Catch you later, Jen."

She sat for a while watching him walk away. None of it made sense. Why did Alan Colder wait until his death bed to tell his sons about the robbery?

Jen did a u-turn and headed back into town.

There had to be something she was missing. Five minutes later she parked her mother's hatchback in Court Street across the road from the Police Station. Up ahead she spotted Senior Constable Abby Taylor striding down the street, her blonde hair was pulled back into neat bun.

Perfect.

Jen climbed out of her car. "Hey, Abby, you got a minute?"

Abby looked up and waved back. Jen ran across the road to join her.

"I know you're busy, but I've just spoken to Brock Coldwell and he's admitted that it was his brother, Gareth, who did the graffiti on Laurie's car. Can we do anything?"

Abby flashed a piercing gaze. "What were you doing there at this hour to find that out?"

Jen face fell. She hadn't expected to be questioned. "I challenged him. I've been digging around and discovered his father was one of the robbers. Alan Colt is their father."

Abby nodded. "Thanks Jen, I've got to run. I'll speak to Laurie about it and I might have a chat with the boys later on."

"Great. Thanks Abby."

Jen stood for quite a while processing progress. So far so good.

***

"What time do you call this?"

Laurie's voice reverberated down the small hallway. Jennifer raced along it and gave him a quick nod as she passed his office. "Sorry, Laurie. I got caught in traffic. I forgot it's market day on the Monday holiday."

"How long have you lived here? You should know what's going on like the back of your hand."

Jen slid into her chair and grimaced to Mel. Laurie's sister shook her head. Jen pulled a new packet of jelly beans out of her bag and emptied it into the jar at her desk. She switched on her laptop.

"Quite a turn-out today," murmured Mel as she glanced across the street at the stalls being set up opposite.

Jen clicked on her emails and watched as the enquiries came through for various properties. It used to excite her looking at all those potential sales, but now she knew they were only curious enquiries and most people needed them to work on their figures for other properties they were purchasing. Sending out the details each day ate into her morning.

She went to the little kitchenette and turned on the kettle. Then she sauntered down to Laurie's office, stood in the doorway and gave a gentle knock on his door.

"Laurie, do you have a minute?"

He looked up and nodded. It had taken a while to get used to his gruff demeanour. It used to scare her, but not anymore.

"Is this about you being made permanent? You keep hounding me. You only asked yesterday."

She stepped into his office. "Well. I thought it might help if we set down a date and time to discuss it." Jen winced at the high pitch of her voice, and hoped it didn't sound like she was begging, but without a permanent job her life was essentially on hold.

Laurie leaned back in his chair and rubbed his face. "I'm still thinking about it. I know you want an answer."

She bit her bottom lip. What would it take?

Laurie let out a few noisy sighs, but didn't say a word.

Jen didn't just want an answer. She needed an answer. Being nice and patient to everyone did not work. It didn't pay the bills or get her where she wanted to go.

She pulled out the chair opposite his desk and sat down.

"You won't get anybody more experienced than me. I've been in sales all my working life, worked at the coffee shop, pulled beers at the pub, have done the bookkeeping for Hannah McKenna and I've run my own make-up business, so I'm very sales and people oriented. Most people in town know me."

Laurie stared at her. His face remained unmoved.

Eventually his silent message got through to Jen. She took her time in getting out of her chair because she still wanted to give him as long as he needed to respond. He looked tired, but she was over waiting. She couldn't do this much longer, this living in hope.

"I'll let you know soon." His dismissive tone said more than his words. His tone hurt. How long's a piece of string? She so wanted to challenge him. Another time.

As she stood up it dawned on her. At each of her past jobs she'd given each of them the same speech, hoping, wanting, needing to be made permanent, and it wasn't working for her.

He flicked her a short sharp look. "Jen, sorry, the timing's just not right at the moment."

She nodded. She bit back saying *'it's okay, not a problem'*. They were her go-to words for these situations. Instead, she walked out without a backward glance.

Enough.

What would it take to get over the line?

She'd started her make-up business in the hope that she could dispense with such an embarrassing, almost begging, speech, but there weren't too many calls for make-up parties in Bindarra Creek. Her main orders were replacement lipsticks and a few odd pieces.

Back in the kitchenette, she wondered if people took her seriously. Silly question; they didn't. With her job record she was everybody's fallback when things got busy, but in the quiet times, nobody called her.

Where did it get her, being so nice and helpful?

She grabbed the coffees, dropped one on Laurie's desk; one on Mel's and sat down at her desk with her own. While her mind churned over what to do next she glanced across at the market.

Mel stood up and straightened her skirt. "I've put in an order for some strawberry jam. I'll just pop over. Won't be a tick."

Jen watched Mel as she walked across the road. In seconds she'd disappeared into the growing crowd. Further down Jen spotted the Colder brothers. She sat bolt upright, took a sip of her coffee and studied them as they checked out the tables. She couldn't imagine what would interest them in a market.

Then she heard it. A familiar cry.

JoJo.

She stood up and stared through the glass door. Torn between rushing out to search for JoJo and holding the fort for Laurie, she searched the crowd for JoJo's familiar red dress. She spotted a red blur flashing between people – it was JoJo, but without Jen's mother. Without hesitation Jen put down her coffee, pushed open the door and ran across the road. She kept her eye on aunt, surprised at the older lady's speed. JoJo was not weaving between people but running at full speed ahead, pushing her way through. Jen spotted Cleopatra, JoJo's favourite doll, in JoJo's arms, the doll's feet catching the overlapping table cloths of each table. At the final table of books and magazines, Cleopatra's foot snagged on the edge of the table cloth. Most of the books and magazines tipped onto the footpath.

As fast as her legs could carry her Jen pushed her way past the small crowd and made a grab at JoJo's red dress, but it slipped through her fingers.

"JoJo, stop. Stop."

Out of the corner of her eye Jen saw a dark figure move in. He blocked her view and for a moment she lost sight of JoJo.

Then she heard the familiar wail.

Jen ran around the man. He was holding JoJo firmly with his hands on her shoulders, pinning her to the spot.

"Hey, hey, it's okay. You're okay." His soothing voice carried some weight. JoJo's eyes were glued on the man, a wondrous expression blooming across her face.

Jen glanced at Brock Colder. In seconds her brain computed his snug-fit jeans and t-shirt which emphasised every muscle and movement of his body. The man was a walking, talking advertisement for fitness.

Jen understood her aunt's expression. Not many muscled men rocked up to JoJo to get close and personal. She slid her arms around JoJo's slight shoulders.

"Come here, JoJo. What's upset you, eh?" Her aunt's eyes never left Brock and her body was hard, solid, like some immovable cast-iron stature, as she held Cleopatra close to her chest. Jen reached around and rubbed her aunt's back. She kept up with a gentle rock in an effort to warm her, to calm her down.

Her eyes were drawn to Brock. He didn't seem at all put out given their earlier conversation. "Thank you. I don't know what happened there. Something set her off."

He started to respond when Jen's mother burst into the scene. "Oh, you're here. Thank god, you caught her." She shuffled towards them, her face flush from the effort. Her mother's heavy wheezing was a shock to Jen. "Jen, get back to work, we're alright here."

Jen gave a quick look around. There had to be a trigger somewhere. JoJo never left her mother's side.

Her mother's eyes flitted across to Brock, then back at Jen. "Jen, your job's important. Get back to work."

She held up her hands. "Okay. I'll call you later."

Jen turned to leave when Mel came up, her eyes surveying the scene. "I'll deal with Laurie. Take an early lunch; this is family. It's okay. Trust me."

Jen nodded, and then sidled up to her mother. "What were you thinking? I thought all you had to do was take some more dolls to the library."

The local library's idea for a planned exhibit, *Local Dolls & Toys since Bindarra Creek's settlement* sounded great when first raised. They hadn't yet confirmed any dates because they wanted to see the dolls and toys before committing to do the exhibit. Each week JoJo kept adding another one of her dolls. For months she wouldn't agree for any of her dolls to be on display. Lately, she'd changed her mind.

Conscious of Brock standing beside her, Jen grinned up at him. "Life has its moments."

She turned to her mother. "Mum, this is Brock Colder; he's repairing the car damage."

Her mother looked up and gave him a weary smile. "Nice to meet you, Brock. I'm sorry it's not under calmer circumstances."

He shook her mother's hand. "Nice to meet you too, Mrs Rogers. I'll leave you to it and sort out a few things down here."

Jen watched him head towards the book stall where people were milling around sifting the books fallen through broken cardboard boxes.

"He seems nice," her mother murmured. "Is he new in town?"

She nodded. "Yes, and he's not hanging around either. So don't get ideas."

Her mother let out a snort. "Heaven forbid I should get an idea."

No amount of humour could erase the exhaustion or despair from her mother's face.

"I thought you and JoJo were just going to drop the dolls off. What happened?"

Her mother dropped her bags down at Jen's feet. "We were, but I thought if I didn't get here early I might miss out on a few things. I just wanted to have a look-see." Her bottom lip quivered and her tear-filled eyes caught Jen's. "What a mess."

Jen studied the mess and today's incident firmed in her head an idea that had been brewing for a while. It could be the answer. She gave her mother a quick kiss on the cheek and ushered her and JoJo to the side of the building, to stand in the shade. "Come on, stand back here with JoJo and I'll tidy things up around here."

Her mother's body stiffened. "I wasn't talking about the mess in the street, love. Nobody's seen JoJo like that before. I feel she's entertained every family in Bindarra Creek for weeks. You can imagine, can't you?"

Jen swallowed hard. Her mother treasured her privacy. This public exposure would be ripping her apart. "Mum, relax. It's done. People are pretty tolerant and understand these days."

Her mother shot her a quick glance. "Are they?"

Further down the street she could see Brock helping restore order to a few stalls that JoJo's charge had put into disarray. She also saw Laurie standing in the doorway opposite.

A firm hand squeezed her upper arm. She turned. Florrie Miller gave her a gentle smile. "You better head back to work, love. I'll take your mum and JoJo over the street for a nice cup of tea and cake. What about it?"

Florrie to the rescue. She smiled at the vicar. "Oh, Florrie, thanks. That's just what Mum needs right now."

Her mother took JoJo's hand. "We're good, love. I see Laurie looking out for you."

She kissed JoJo and her mother, and then squeezed the older woman's arm. "Florrie, will you be at the pub later tonight? There's something I've been meaning to run by you."

Florrie gave her a quizzical look. "Of course, I'll see you later."

On Jen's return trip to the office, she veered toward the stalls where Brock was helping tidy the mess. Jen didn't hesitate to bend down and pick up a nearby fallen table cloth. The lace cloth, caught around the table's base, managed somehow not to tear.

As she folded it up she watched Brock, the largest man in the street and a hard one to ignore. He was rearranging some jam jars. His whole body moved in one fluid motion. She tried hard not to stare and failed. He looked good from his feet all the way up to his handsome head.

Jen's ears tingled; a warm feeling pulsed over them. *Someone's talking about me.* Laurie. He could wait another minute.

She went over to Brock.

"Brock, thanks for all your help. Please, leave this. I'll deal with it."

"All good. Anyway I think it's almost done. Everything's back in place."

"How long you staying in town?" She blushed. They'd been through this. "I mean today, today in town." Her mind crashed and burned as she took in the amusement in his eyes, the slight lift of an eyebrow, not to mention the curious lift of his lips. He was affecting her in all the wrong places. Yep, the silly season was here, she could not take her eyes off the man as she noted every move he made no matter how slight.

"Jen, are you free now?"

Mel. Damn. Why do these things always happen to me? Jen dragged her eyes away from Brock to Mel who stood waving to her.

"Work's calling. I've got to go." Jen nodded to Brock and made a bee-line direct to Mel.

Inside, Mel grimaced. "Sorry, Jen. Laurie's got another Q&A starting soon."

The afternoon flew in a flurry of coffee drop-offs to the boardroom Laurie used for his Q&A sessions, running out to buy cakes and milk, printing more handouts, printing out more maps of Bindarra Creek and keeping the jug full of water. Her "Welcome to Laurie's Realty" smile was now a permanent fixture on her face.

Jen eyed the clock in Laurie's office as she waited while he signed a few letters. They had thirty more minutes to go before the madness ended.

The doorbell rang. Moments later Mel popped her head around the door. "Laurie, two guys are here to see you."

Laurie didn't miss a beat. "Jen, will you take them to the small boardroom? I'll be finished with these in a minute."

In the hallway, she heard familiar voices and peered down the corridor into reception. In front of the reception desk, chatting to Mel, were Brock and Gareth.

Jen back-tracked to Laurie. "Laurie, the two guys are Brock and Gareth Colder. They're the ones I took the car to for the respray; they're the ones renting out Reg's garage. I gave them my card that morning."

She hesitated.

Laurie looked up. "Is there something else?"

She nodded and closed his door. "It's a matter of confidentiality. Brock told me Gareth damaged the car."

Laurie handed her the signed letters. "Thanks, Jen. Abby called me earlier this morning about that. I'm not going to press any changes."

Jen hung back. "Also, Brock viewed the one-bedder upstairs and I'm not sure Gareth knows about that. He could."

Laurie nodded. "Gotcha. I won't say a word. Thank you, Jen. I'll be there in a minute."

She walked into reception and hid her surprise. The Colder brothers together were an intimidating package and she kept her "*Welcome to Laurie's Realty*" smile in place as she joined Mel. Her eyes were drawn to Gareth. His ready-made smile had an edge to it, almost a challenge. He nodded to her, and his eyes flashed a warning.

Those guys sent her a message. Brock was maybe the softer one, but they shared the same blood. These brothers were a tag team. Hell, these guys meant business.

Set yourself on fire.

She stepped forward and nodded to Gareth. He needed the attention.

"Nice to see you both again. Come this way."

***

"I want us in and out. The fewer questions the better. Got it?"

Brock ignored his brother's words, spoken before they stepped into the agency. He studied Jen as she walked across to them; her beaming smile went straight to Gareth. Something about that irked him. Brock shouldered past his brother and followed Jen into the small reception area.

"Laurie Chester's the principal at this agency and he won't be a moment. Can I get you coffee, water?" Her smile flashed bright at them, almost as if she'd brushed aside the upheaval outside.

Laurie bustled into the room, papers in hand. He shook both their hands. "Gentlemen, I'm Laurie Chester. I don't think we've met. It's Gareth and Brock Colder? I didn't expect to see you here today. Jen tells me you're respraying the car. How's it coming along?"

Brock sat down by the window. "It'll be another couple of days before we can start. We'll start sourcing the paint tomorrow, once this long weekend's over."

Laurie nodded. "If you don't mind I'd like Jen to be part of this meeting. She can take down some notes. You okay with that?"

Both men nodded.

Brock kept his eyes on her. Jen spun around, her soft blonde hair falling over her face as she stepped outside for a notebook. She returned and sat beside Laurie.

"Right. What can we do for you?'

Gareth pushed forward. He wore his usual flashy grin. "We're looking for a small shop front to lease. Preferably on Main Street, if possible."

Laurie picked up a pen, his eyes steady on Gareth. "A small shop front? What business?"

Brock hated subterfuge; he knew his brother was messing them about. He had no intention of leasing anything. "We plan to open up a tattoo parlour."

Gareth tapped the table, his fingers in a steady heavy rhythm on the wooden surface.

Brock wanted to get out of that room. He was sanctioning Gareth's outright lie. He studied Laurie as his eyes checked out both their arms and neck. The man's not a fool. Neither of them had a tat.

Laurie nodded. "That's different for up this way. Are you guys artists, or will you be bringing one in?"

"We're working on details now. Probably bring one in," responded Gareth.

Laurie slammed shut his book. "Good, then. We'll get back to you soon about it. I'm sure you want to enjoy the last of the long weekend."

Brock took his time walking out of the office. He spied Jen and the receptionist chatting in the hallway, sharing a laugh. Laurie's voice, strong and firm filtered down the hallway. Laurie looked to be a guy in his early thirties, but he liked the man's quiet confidence. He was working on his business and on his future. How would it feel to work at a business, to build it up and see it grow?

Brock's work history was sketchy at best and he'd enjoyed the odd beer with colleagues. He fitted in, worked hard and moved on.

Where was it getting him?

Chapter Twelve

On dusk, Jen sat in her car mother's hatchback in the Riverside carpark. So far no sign of Taylah or Florrie, but she could wait. *Success isn't a result of spontaneous combustion. You must set yourself on fire.* Those words in Laurie's office played out in her mind. Her father always said, *You can do anything once you set your mind to it.* True, but so far it hadn't given her any form of success.

Jen considered herself fairly easy to get along with, and flexible when she contemplated all the different roles she'd taken on for work. For some roles she'd turned herself inside out at times to learn a new skill, to earn tips, to work with colleagues she couldn't stand, and to get a good reference for the next job. It wore her out.

She sat up as Laurie strode through the carpark and into the pub, followed by Mel who did a little run behind him to keep up. Laurie slapped some papers against his thigh as he gesticulated to a tired and frazzled Mel. He never stopped working. *He's on fire,* she mused. They were having a casual business meeting without her. Hurt and disappointment shunted through her.

She should change tack and stop working at ways to change, to fit in. Nobody noticed her. She could save people money, do a great job and still nobody would notice her.

A black shiny four-wheel drive drove past and parked three cars away.

Her interest piqued, she watched Brock and Gareth climb out. Jen studied Brock with his easy confidence and smooth, efficient movements. She could watch him all day; from any angle, the man looked good.

What were they *really* doing in a town like this?

Curious, she kept her eye on the brothers, studying them through her car's rear-vision mirror as they walked towards the pub's entry. At the doorway Brock turned, his gaze gravitating toward her. Their eyes locked and her treacherous eyes held his gaze. He lifted an arm and waved her to come over.

She didn't move.

He pointed to her.

She pointed to herself. - *Me?* - even though there wasn't another soul in her car.

With a hint of a playful stern expression, which caused a warm rush over Jen's skin, Brock nodded.

A smile broke out over her face. Yep, he meant her.

Should she go? Apart from her brain's hesitation, every other part of her body didn't care. One step at a time took her right to him.

He stood aside and let her walk in front of him. His fingers touched lightly against her back steering her towards the bar, and sending an excited tingle right through her. They still hadn't had a drink, the man hadn't yet spoken to her, and yet she was having the most fun in a very long time.

Inside she spotted Gareth having an animated conversation with Laurie and Mel.

Brock pulled out a stool for her.

"What can I get you?" he asked. His simple question sent her mind doing loops about how best to answer it. Who knew where a cheeky answer would land her? She held her lips firm instead.

He leaned closer, so close his five o'clock shadow was a slight touch away. "A cocktail, or wine?"

"A mocktail, please."

Brock nodded to the waiter at the end of the bar.

The waiter came by and slammed two drinks menus in front of them. "Cocktails at the front, we do virgin-style mocktails, if you want, and the wines are on the back."

Brock moved a little closer to her, and handed back the menus to the waiter. He glanced across at her, amusement written all over his face. "We'll go virgin-style, eh?"

His willingness to anticipate her needs warmed her belly. "I'd like that."

He raised an eyebrow and her belly got a little warmer. She fought hard to keep her emotions in check. "The pomegranate-lime sounds good."

His eyes never left her face. "Good. We'll both have that."

The back door to the pub opened and she looked through into the garden courtyard. Her favourite time of day, dusk, wasn't far off. The outdoor lights hadn't yet come on, but she could smell the faint scent of a barbeque.

He picked up their drinks. "Come on, let's find a table somewhere to people-watch."

They settled for a small table by the side wall out of view of Laurie, Gareth and Mel. Jen took a sip of the sweet, cold drink. "Thank you. That is a seriously nice drink."

He grimaced as he shone it in front of the light. "It is; for virgin-style, it's got enough punch."

From their table opposite the bar, Jen noticed couples were starting to pour into the place. Lucky it was a Monday night, it wouldn't be as rowdy as the weekend.

"What brings you to Bindarra Creek? Most people pass through."

Almost instantly she regretted asking him. She knew - the jewellery. Jen took another sip of her drink and studied Brock. He didn't seem at all fazed by her question. She couldn't detect any change in him.

Brock looked thoughtful. "We pass through most towns. We've never laid down roots. We're wanderers. Our family pulls up in a new town, gives it a couple of seasons and then moves on. But we're going to split up soon. Gareth's headed for Sydney. He's an accountant and there's a few job prospects there for him."

"And you?"

He shook his head. "Sydney doesn't do it for me. I wouldn't know what to do with myself in a big city. I'd miss the bush."

"You must be considering Bindarra Creek if you're interested in leasing a shop front."

Whoops! Oh, if she could only catch those words and put them back in their box. She went still. Don't get involved. *He's plotting against you.*

"Not sure, yet. Might decide after we get a business up and running."

"What are you looking for?"

His eyes locked on hers. "Fun."

She stared at her drink.

He leaned closer. "Fun, pure and simple."

Her body heated in that instant. *That's it. He's way out of my league.* Jen laid her glass on the table before she spilt it. "You mean on the wild side, don't you? A bit of fun on the side? Before you up and leave?"

His gaze held firm. "I was being polite. That too."

His words blew her mind as his mellow voice purred over her. There was no mistaking his intention.

Jen looked away as she collected her thoughts. As she suspected, he just wanted a bit of fun on the side. Disappointment drifted over her.

She turned back to him. "Do you play a sport? Sports are very big in Bindarra Creek. You can join any club you fancy."

Brock burst out laughing, a deep rumble erupting from his chest.

She loved it. "Sorry, you lucked out on the wild side with me."

He arched a brow. "I don't think I have. You can only hide for so long."

With a twinkle in his eye Brock picked up their empty glasses and sauntered across to the bar.

Was that right? Was he seeing something in her that others weren't? She shouldn't get ahead of herself; the man was dangerous on every level.

"Well, somebody looks happy with themselves." Like a splash of ice-cold water Florrie Miller's voice cut through her thoughts.

Jen looked up to see Florrie looking mildly amused at her. She squirmed. Thank god the woman couldn't read her thoughts.

Out of the corner of her eye she saw Brock nod to her from the bar.

Florrie followed her gaze. "I see. He's the young man who helped clean things up this morning."

"Yes, he's Brock Colder. He's leasing out Reg's old mechanic's workshop with his brother, Gareth."

Together they watched as Brock navigated his way toward them carrying three cocktails and one glass of water.

He beamed at them. "Three pomegranate-limes, virgin-style, and a glass of water if it's too much."

Florrie let out a gentle laugh. "Oh, my, I'm going to enjoy this. Thank you, Brock."

"Cheers," announced Jen, feeling rather smug. "Brock, meet Florrie Miller, she's our local vicar."

"Lovely to meet you, Florrie."

Florrie nodded. "Likewise, Brock." Her warm gaze moved across to Jen. "Now tell me, young lady, are you free to chat now, or later?"

Jennifer swallowed hard. In the warmth of her cosy bed where all her thoughts lined up, everything had seemed possible; now face to face with Florrie, her thoughts were a jumble where doubts about her idea flourished. *Keep it simple.*

"Well, there are child-minding centres for children. Could we have one for people with dementia, people who are classified as high-care, like JoJo? Only for about two mornings a week, just to give carers a break? I've been looking into it. Mum needs a rest and a couple of hours' break a week would help. So she can get her hair cut, do a bit of shopping, have a catch-up with friends, do something on her own, without JoJo tagging along."

Jen slumped down in her chair, glad her idea was out.

Florrie took her hand and squeezed it. Relief trickled through Jen when she saw the compassion in Florrie's eyes.

"Well?" she asked.

"I like it. I know a few families in the same predicament. Not everybody is prepared to let their loved ones go into a nursing home."

Jen reached across and took a sip of her cocktail. "I've searched, we could apply to the government to get a specialist nurse in, and we'd have to find somewhere safe. Even one day a month would help."

"I can see this taking off," said Florrie.

"How will you fund it?" asked Brock. His question forced her to reveal the other half of her plan. It sounded way out there, but it might work.

"Always the tricky part," murmured Florrie.

"I wondered if we could have an auction. What if we auctioned twelve first dates tickets to a barbeque at the McKenna's because they have that big verandah out the back? What do you think?"

Florrie's eyes widened. "What made you think of that?"

Jen's lips quivered into a smile. "You did, Florrie. You mentioned musical chairs the other day and I thought we could do something similar, but swap seats at every course. Get my drift?"

Leaning in closer, Brock's broad chest bumped her upper arm. "I sure do and I love the idea. When can I buy a ticket?"

Jen's heart thudded in her chest. She turned to Florrie. "Well, what do you think?"

Florrie leaned back, a cheeky grin on her face. "I think it has legs. Let's ask the question. When the DJ starts tonight, how about you hop up first and test the waters and ask the crowd what they think? Get some feedback?"

Jen made a show of looking horrified. "Oh, no, Florrie, can't you? Everybody listens to you."

"You should," said Brock. "Speak from the heart, you can do that. Only you can, you know it firsthand. Remember, speak from the heart."

Could she do that?

Chapter Thirteen

Brock handed his empty plate to the waitress. Gareth's plan for them to have a quick drink at the local had gone south the moment they walked in. For once his brother didn't get his way and as always a small part of Brock cheered. Being new in town, they hadn't expected to eat a meal with so many - Jen, Taylah, Florrie, old Reg, Laurie and his sister, Melissa.

Gareth shot him a knowing look. Brock saw the warning and knew his brother itched to leave, but not yet. It seemed years since they'd sat down for a meal with such a great bunch of people, and Brock liked it.

Reg nudged him. "Hey mate, Jen tells me I'm too old to buy a ticket to this first dates thing. I fancy my chances there."

Jen laughed out loud. "Reg Myles, I reckon you've had more first dates than you've had hot dinners and I don't think you can afford the moderns girls. You're such a tight wad. You won't be fooling any of them."

Reg let out a laugh which ended in a spluttering cough.

"Now, Reg, calm yourself," said Florrie. "At your age you should zip it."

Reg let out another belly laugh, and then made out to zip his mouth. "I hear you, Florrie."

Florrie turned to Jen. "Are you going to make an announcement? You need to get an idea of the level of interest."

Jen nodded, the end of her blonde ponytail bouncing at the back of her neck.

"I'm not making any announcement, I'm going to go to each table and ask the question, maybe even get some suggestions. Who knows?"

Florrie nodded as she settled in beside Reg. "Okay. Keep me posted."

Jen pulled out a notepad from her bag and then gave a little twirl as she held up a pen. "I'm armed and ready. I'll take some notes. Won't be long."

Brock sat back with the strange sensation of unease. That feeling only came when he listened to any of Gareth's plans, but with Jen around, another kind of unease grew. He was in unfamiliar territory.

Reg tapped him on the arm. "Watch that one, she's a keeper. I found one or two in my time and let them go. Bloody fool."

His landlord's words hit a nerve. The old boy, dressed in a clean, baggy pair of jeans and an old tartan shirt that had seen better days, gave him a toothless grin. Sincerity beamed from the man's lined, but well-scrubbed, face. Brock didn't doubt his sincerity.

Reg loved his cars, especially the early models from the 1950s. Despite the dust and rust on the sheds, on the inside he'd spent good money in his day on getting the best equipment and parts for them.

Brock could feel himself getting sucked in. He was fast getting too comfortable with these people.

"Yes, she's a keeper," murmured Reg.

Brock's gaze flew to Jen, who stood at a nearby table chatting to a group of four. A keeper. Brock knew the old sentiment well. A keeper, something about that word sounded like a ball and chain, but was it?

All this would end in grief. Gareth would not leave town without those jewels.

The more Brock mixed with the locals, the more the problems compounded.

Brock hated lying and they were lying to everyone they met - right from the get-go, when Jen had asked him what his plans were. He couldn't share their plans with anyone. *His* plan remained the same, to find the jewels to get his brother off his back. He wanted to be free of his past and his domineering brother.

Then what? He shifted in his chair, unsure of where his thoughts were going.

Between tables Jen turned, caught his eye. He gave her a return wink.

Brock in his heart knew he should back off, but some-how he just kept dipping his toe into trouble.

He followed Jen's progress from table to table. He knew the minute he laid eyes on her she was a real gem, a sweet-heart. He loathed not playing it straight with her, or any-one else. If ever she found out what he and Gareth were up to, she'd walk.

He downed the last of the iced water for their table and vowed to enjoy his time with them. Best to move on and start somewhere fresh, untarnished.

Then he saw it. Some jerk's hand, half a dozen tables away, skimmed over Jen's behind. She froze and jumped away.

Brock stood up, his eyes fixed on the jerk.

Gareth saw it too and, being closer, rose to his feet and strode across to Jen's side.

"You're getting a little close there, sport," growled Gareth.

The guy nodded, his eyes widening as he spied Brock close behind Gareth. His friends pushed away from their table, all the time their eyes glued on the brothers.

Brock's stance hardened. "You guys leaving?"

The jerk stood up. He grimaced at Jen. "Sorry. I didn't mean anything by it. Don't want any trouble. We'll go."

Brock stood back with Gareth by his side as the four guys stood up. He and Gareth took one step closer, forcing the guys to walk past them on their way out of the pub. All four stank of beer and sweat. Brock couldn't help noting their faces for future reference.

He sucked in a deep breath, disgusted with himself. These guys were just trying it on. Some street habits were hard to drop.

"Thank you both," gushed Jen. "That's rare around here. I just think he had a little too much to drink, you know?"

Brock met Jen's anxious eyes. He got it. In her world she worked hard to make things right. "I know you're letting him off the hook. He was just a tad too familiar, eh?"

She nodded. "I think I'll call it a night. It's been good."

"Hey Jen," called out Reg. "Many takers for the first date auction?"

Her face lit up. "You betcha! Everybody liked the idea. Florrie, I'll make a few calls about what we do to get a nurse here, and I'll ask the Council about finding a safe place. I'm sure we're going to have to meet them half-way or make an offer to help fund it."

Florrie gathered her things. "You'll need to write a submission to them. I'll go through it with you."

"Thank you."

Laurie stood up, rubbing his hands together. "Right, then. Let's call it a night. We all have early starts."

"Yeah, right behind you, Laurie," sang out Reg.

Minutes later, they all stood outside in the cool breeze. The cloudless sky was smothered with stars. The cool breeze woke Brock, shook him up out of his reverie.

He kept his distance, watching as they said their good-byes. They all stood in the small sheltered entrance still chatting. He knew the feeling; none of them were quite ready to call the night quits. Their goodbyes went on forever. Finally Laurie and Mel moved on and the others continued to chat.

Making the most of the congenial atmosphere he rocked back and forth on the balls of his feet.

"Jen, I meant to ask earlier."

He could feel her eyes on him. The goodbyes ceased and all eyes turned to him. In the ensuing silence, he changed tack and shifted his feet, left to right and back again. His timing was off. This couldn't get any harder. Jen gave him a nod of encouragement.

He puffed out a sigh. "We're getting some business in. Do you know any part-time bookkeepers who could do about two hours a couple of times a week? We haven't set anything up, but I think we need someone to start on the books. Or, you? Is that something you can do?"

His body stilled. What had he just done? Where had that idea come from? They were slowly getting some work in, but not enough to require a bookkeeper.

He ignored the sharp intake of breath from Gareth who stood beside him. With a new intensity Brock studied Jen's face.

She gave him a gentle smile. "I'll think about that and let you know. Leave it with me, I won't leave you in the dark for long."

Reg slapped him on the back. "Sounds good, sounds like you've got plans."

Not plans, he wanted to scream. He couldn't put a name to it; maybe he was feeling comfortable with these people. He loved working on cars, especially Reg's. He'd love to do one up for the old boy and get it registered so Reg could drive around town in it. Maybe he did have a plan, he just never thought it through long enough.

Jen smiled at Brock as she waved them all goodbye. "I'll be in touch."

He and Gareth watched them all escape to their cars and drive out of the near empty carpark.

Gareth pulled out his keys and pressed the button. His dark eyes slid across to Brock.

"I never ever saw you as manipulative and conniving. I'm going to have to watch you. Strike one for us. You have put us front and centre. These people will think we're up front and honest. I could not have dreamed that one myself ... a bookkeeper."

With great reluctance Brock followed his brother into Gareth's four-wheel drive, slid in beside him and tugged at his seat belt.

Gareth drove out of the carpark. "Come on, we have some work to do before we hit the deck tonight."

Brock's blood ran cold. He gave his brother a long hard stare. "You're not serious. You can't go ahead with this. Not now, not after tonight."

His brother shrugged.

"We're so close. We're making progress. I don't have a problem with it."

He bit the inside of his mouth, anxious about the coming weeks. They were making friends with these people, gaining their trust and enjoying their company.

"You can't do this to people."

"Truly? Asking Jen to work for us, keeping her away from the homestead, is pure genius. Who knew you had it in you?"

Brock let out a frustrated sigh.

"We have to keep the pressure up. The missing jewels and loot are somewhere. We've got to flush it out."

Chapter Fourteen

J en hit the snooze button at the first buzz, stretched out in her warm bed, then curled up tight for another ten minutes. She took a couple of deep breaths and pulled up her bedcovers to under her chin. Her mind went straight to the Colder brothers. Brock reminded her of her favourite chocolate; hard on the outside, but soft and yummy on the inside.

Gareth, on the other hand, seemed to have it all together with a smooth and controlled manner. She had no doubt he knew his worth. With his ever-ready smile and a quick word, she wondered how he hadn't been snapped up and married years earlier.

Whatever made Brock ask her about the bookkeeping job? Was he asking in a roundabout way to get to know her? Could she take it on? She hated bookkeeping and dreaded the last week each month working overtime to balance Laurie's profit & loss statement.

In the hallway she heard the heavy-footed run of JoJo on the wooden floors. Jen braced herself. JoJo burst into her room, all noise and bustle.

"Molly's missing."

Jen started at her aunt's breathy voice, edgy with urgency.

Jen peeked out from under her blanket. "What?"

JoJo hit her fisted hands against her sides and stomped her feet. "Molly's not here. She never misses breakfast."

Molly, their golden retriever, rarely left their verandah and at fourteen years old she struggled to move fast or far on her arthritic joints.

JoJo's bottom lip trembled. "She's not here. I've called and called."

Jen sat up. "Where's Sam?"

On hearing his name, Sam, their second golden retriever waddled in.

Jen couldn't tame her thoughts. Would Molly have gone somewhere to die? To be on her own? Molly and Sam were the best of mates and as her sight grew worse they'd all seen Sam being very protective of her. He'd never leave her side.

"Have you checked under the house? She's probably having a snooze somewhere."

With a flash of determination in her eyes, JoJo walked over to Jen and in one quick movement pulled the blanket off.

"We've got to find her," she declared.

Jen nodded. "Okay, let's do this," she said as she slipped on her dressing gown and pulled on her runners.

Outside, Jen rubbed her hands against the early morning cold. She tightened the belt on her dressing gown and knelt down to pat a sleepy looking Sam who'd followed them.

"Where's Molly?" Jen looked into Sam's big brown trusting eyes and kissed him on the forehead. "We'll find her."

The morning was clear, no sign of mist, giving her a good view across the paddocks. She almost willed Molly, with her clumsy lop-sided gait and wagging tail, to come out and join them, but she suspected they would find her body. Together she and JoJo searched inside her father's sheds, the long grasses around the top half of the dam and the back verandah of the old homestead, a favourite haunt of both dogs.

At every stage JoJo muttered to herself and ran on ahead.

Something caught her eye by the old Rose garden in the distance, something grey, and then it disappeared. What would that be? Ever since she'd seen Brock and Gareth walk Main Street counting steps she saw trouble in everything.

Still, she did see something, a grey something moving.

"JoJo," she called and pointed toward the old driveway leading to the private road the family never used. JoJo nodded, stumbled as she changed direction and ran on ahead. As her aunt picked up speed Jen started to run. Her heart beat faster as she followed her aunt down the narrow driveway.

JoJo veered right and ran through the long wet grasses which framed the old driveway. Jen followed her and in seconds the bottoms of her pyjama legs were damp and smothered in grass seeds. Ignoring any discomfort, they continued to run down the slope toward the main gate post with the old letter box still sitting on top of it.

Her heart raced and her breath caught in her throat as she kept her eye on JoJo's fast disappearing figure. How could a woman JoJo's age out-pace and out-run her?

A high-pitched shriek rang out.

At the sound Jen stumbled, regained her footing and carried on running.

No, no, no, no, no.

On the final turn, Jen slid on the wet grasses and fell. She hauled herself up and ran down the few metres left of the path until she reached JoJo.

Her aunt sat sobbing and hunched on the ground by Molly, who lay at the base of the gate post.

When she reached her aunt's side Jen slid down beside her and wrapped her arms about JoJo's thin shoulders. With her other arm she slipped her hand under Sam's collar to keep a firm hold of him. She held them both close to her side.

Jen studied the beautiful and faithful Molly, who lay fully stretched out before them. Despite half expecting to find her dead, it still took a few minutes to resonate in her head that Molly was gone.

She sat back. Molly was old but it was strange that she was this far from the homestead.

What's happened?

How did she get here? Molly never left home. Jen wondered if Molly's death was not old age – maybe not even an accident. The silent words screamed in Jen's head. Even if she'd been bitten by a snake Molly wouldn't be this far from home. Why only Molly? Is Sam next?

She ruffled Sam's neck and his warmth and soft body provided some comfort. Jen let go of a sniffling JoJo, who continued to murmur Molly's name.

She ached to gather Molly in her arms for one of their big shake hugs. Her eyes brimmed with tears as she shrugged off her dressing gown and laid it across Molly's body. Her thin pyjamas held no protection against the cool morning air. She shivered. Jen pulled her aunt close to her and together they stood until JoJo pulled back.

"Shouldn't we say a prayer?"

Jen nodded at her aunt's softly spoken words.

"Morning, I didn't expect to see anybody here this early."

The friendly words cut across their thoughts. Stunned, she and JoJo turned at the sound of the familiar voice.

What?

Brock stood at the end of their driveway, not twelve metres away, dressed in jeans and runners with a grey hoodie over his head. In his arms lay Jasper, squirming and wriggling, itching to be free.

Her body refused to move as a few unwelcome thoughts started to dominate and a horrifying theme emerged. This man walked Main Street and stopped when he'd counted one hundred and fifty steps. Molly was dead at the letter box marked one hundred and fifty. Now, he's hanging around the letter box marked one hundred and fifty.

He and Gareth mean business.

That thought left her cold as she took in his handsome face, his skin pink, glowing as only a peaches and cream complexion can, bordered by a dark five o'clock shadow.

Jen took her time to gather her thoughts while she bent her head down to grab Sam's collar. She gave a quick glance at Molly and struggled to contain her emotions. She did not want things to get difficult between them and she'd think about the implications later.

With a steely resolve she pulled away from her aunt and kept a tight rein on a curious Sam. She walked across to the dusty driveway and down to the property's entry point.

"What are you doing here, Brock? This is a private road."

Her harsh voice and blunt words hit home. He did a double-take and his eyes widened in surprise. Brock pulled back his hoodie, revealing his messed hair.

"Sorry, I didn't realise. I've been taking Jasper for a walk every morning down these little back lanes trying to map out the area."

His eyes roamed over her body and Jen fought back the urge to soften her stance. She didn't really know Brock and right now her gut wires were crossed. Not for the first time did she wish she had a sibling to share things with. How good would it be to have a brother or sister beside her now?

She hated confrontation. Jen waved her arms in the direction of the McKenna property, the homestead's roofline merging with the rising sun.

"Brock, you should be careful in these back lanes. These are working farms around here and you should keep Jasper on a leash. Most properties have a guard dog to protect cattle and prize-winning horses."

Brock stepped closer to her, the frown on his brow deepening. "Is everything okay?"

Surprised at the intimacy in his voice, she shook her head. "No, it isn't," she whispered. "We've just found our beautiful Molly dead. We had two beautiful older goldies."

Unease rippled down Jen's spine as she studied his every movement while his eyes wandered over to an upset JoJo, who still stood by Molly.

She waited, every part of her body on alert for a sign of some kind.

He grimaced. "I'm so sorry. That's never easy. Can I help? Can I carry Molly back?"

She hesitated. The warmth in his voice caught her off-guard. Behind her JoJo continued to sob. With a vehemence she'd never known before, she shook her head.

"No, I'll do it. She's ours and I'll take her home." She spat the words out and Brock flinched.

Instantly she regretted her tone. It struck her she'd never thanked him for the offer, but things had moved on. "I'm sorry, Brock. There's a lot going on right now."

He glanced across at JoJo. "I understand. Things get difficult."

She walked backwards to JoJo, her gaze never leaving Brock.

"Jen, I'm sorry about Molly. I really am. Let me know, please, if there's anything I can do."

Her father's words when training a difficult horse came to mind of going 'softly, softly'. She'd never thought much about the words, but right now, those words meant something.

Jen gave Brock a quick smile, but it didn't go far enough. She didn't have the energy for anything more.

"Thanks, Brock. I appreciate it. It's been a difficult morning. Molly rarely leaves our verandah and I can't figure out what's happened here. She never comes down this far."

He fell silent. Looked away and then back at her. His dark blue eyes seemed to pierce right through to her soul. She held his gaze.

"What do you think happened?"

She ran a hand through her hair. "No idea, but I can't hang around here much longer. I have to get ready for work."

Jasper won his fight and tumbled out of Brock's arms and as quick as, Brock pulled out a lead from his back pocket and secured Jasper to the lead. "How will your father take Molly back? It's a fair distance back to your home."

"His truck."

Brock glanced across to Molly. "That's not very nice." In one swoop Brock picked up Jasper and walked across to JoJo. "JoJo, do you mind holding Jasper while I carry Molly back? We'll put her back to bed and make her comfortable."

JoJo's mouth fell open as she stared up at Brock. In silence she held her arms as Brock handed her a squirming, Jasper.

Brock walked across to Molly, still covered with Jen's pink dressing gown. "Ladies, are we okay to do this?"

Jen nodded.

JoJo gave Brock a shy smile. "Yes."

Jen stood back as Brock knelt down and very gently lifted Molly into his arms and started to carry her to the homestead. JoJo walked alongside him.

A few paces in, JoJo turned, her eyes shiny and bright. "He's nice."

Jen mouthed *I know* to her aunt. His presence made her wonder about how much he knew. Were the brothers involved in Molly's death? She suspected he'd been lurking in the back road knowing they'd find her. Why did he want to be there for that? Why would he care?

She heard the quiet chat between JoJo and Brock.

JoJo let out a giggle and hugged Jasper tight.

Jen quickened her pace to join them. The man has a good heart.

Chapter Fifteen

Three days later Jen turned her car onto Main Road and her eyes shot to Laurie's new street sign. His sign flashed "*Laurie Chester's Realty*" in ten second intervals. The garish, narrow bright yellow and blue sign stood atop the shop awning, hinged to the second floor wall and as high as the top of that floor's window. It was hard to ignore.

The sign might be garish, but upon seeing it, an instant calm descended over her. Laurie might be the biggest pain in her life, but work provided a wonderful escape from the dramas at home.

She steeled herself for the day ahead. In her mind they hadn't fully resolved the long overdue question of Laurie making her permanent. Jen's mind ran through her to-do list for the day. Satisfied she hadn't forgotten anything, she eased her foot on the brake, drove into the narrow car park and parked her mother's hatchback beside Laurie's. She climbed out' dragging her briefcase, shoulder bag and shopping bag with her. She slammed the car door shut and

straightaway heard Laurie's strident tone. Despite him being deep inside the premises, his voice reverberated around
the small carpark.

"The printer's not working, again. Could somebody
please put in a call?"

Laurie looked up at Jen as he made his way back to his
office. His expression grim. "Morning, Jen. What time do
you call this?"

She stalled in the hallway. "Eight thirty?"

Laurie shook his head. "Get your watch fixed. When you
get yourself settled will you pop in please?"

Not wasting another minute, she hot-footed it to her
desk.

With practised ease she emptied a new packet of jelly
beans into the glass bowl by her screen, switched on her
PC, ran down to the kitchen and turned on the kettle,
checked the fridge for fresh milk and cheese, and the cupboard, for biscuits.

She then ran down the hallway into the compact store
room, checked the stationary cupboard for paper and
notepads, and as she walked out switched the printer on
at the power point.

Back at her desk she mouthed to Mel, "Am I in trouble?"

Mel shook her head. "No, he just woke up in a bad
mood."

Jen sighed in relief. "Oh, nothing new then."

Mel gave her a sympathetic smile. "I think he's anxious about the re-sprayed car. He wants more of us on the road."

Jen slapped her hand against her forehead. "I forgot. Brock Colder asked me about bookkeeping for them, only a couple of hours a week. I don't have time, is that something you'd be interested in? He's coming today to drop off the car and he's bound to ask."

Mel stapled a few papers together before she looked up. "Yes, I can do that. If he brings them here each week. That's easy done."

"Great, thanks Mel."

Back at her desk, she picked up a pen and notepad and headed to Laurie's office. Laurie collected quotes like people collect sports cards and his personal favourites were mounted on every wall throughout the office. Her favourite hung on the wall behind Laurie's chair by American businessman, Arnold Glasgow, *"Success isn't a result of spontaneous combustion. You must set yourself on fire."*

A full-sized map of Bindarra Creek township and region lay open on his desk. He gave her a steady gaze as she sat in the seat opposite him.

"Look at this map. You know it? How many times do you study it?"

Is this a trick question? Jen glanced down at the familiar map. She knew it so well she could draw it freehand any time he liked.

She frowned. "Probably not often enough?"

Laurie sat back looking pleased with himself.

"We're living in a golden age. People in Sydney can work from home and they're looking for rural. They're looking for places they can afford, where their children will get a good education, with good sporting facilities. I smell opportunity."

Her mind connected opportunity with unique and she squeezed her fingers around her notepad. Hold on, every month he had another suggestion. She tempered her enthusiasm.

"But, Laurie, their work is still in Sydney, they can't live up here full-time."

Her words didn't dent his eagerness. He lifted his hands and waved away her caution. "That's not our problem. We can solve a huge problem in their life; housing affordability. Sydney's not that far away."

Inside she groaned. "It is if you have to do it every week."

"Who can afford Sydney? We have our own hospital. That map represents a region full of growth and potential. The opportunity is mind-blowing. We're sitting on a possible gold mine here."

The raw energy in his voice almost embarrassed her. Her eyes shot to the poster above Laurie's head 'Set yourself on fire'. The man did live by his aspirations.

"Have there been a lot of inquiries from Sydney?"

He nodded. "Our problem is we're not always up to speed with what's going on. Take the other night at the Riverside. I had a great word with Gareth Colder, a smart man. As you know, they want to lease a shopfront on Main Street. He's also talking about setting up a high-end garage for quality cars in Bindarra Creek. Another opportunity we've got to work on. Those Colder brothers are aiming high. They're good people."

Her mouth fell open. "Why do you say that?"

"Brock mentioned the car is almost finished and he promised at the outset he'd deliver it. The man is good on a promise. Doesn't get any better."

Her heart began to race. "So, they're staying? Permanently?."

Laurie shook his head. "Not sure about that, but we do know they want to open up two separate businesses, a tattoo parlour and a high-end garage. That's smart. They're spreading their financial risk. Brilliant."

Jennifer's mind raced, unsure about this latest revelation. "I thought only bikies opened up tattoo parlours."

Laurie shrugged. "I don't know about that. I'm sure the man has links. I'm not privy to everything."

"They're like ying and yang those brothers," Jen murmured.

Laurie laughed as he started to fold the map. "Good one, Jen. Looks like you're on board. Come on, I'll show you what I want you to do."

Without wanting to ruffle Laurie too much she warmed to his enthusiasm. She followed him down the hall, through reception and out onto the front street.

"You see all these shop fronts? Well, I want you to knock on every door, take a note of everything, date and who you spoke to, and ask them if they are thinking of moving on, or staying on, any plans? You get my drift? And leave them your card."

She groaned. She couldn't think of a worse job. It was tantamount to ratting on her best friends after finding a little inside info about them.

Jen turned to Laurie. "Really?"

"We need info about what's happening in this town. Nobody is knocking on our door with any news, so, we have to ask. You're the perfect person for that. Walk in confident and relaxed, ask to speak to the boss and I'm sure you know who that would be."

She looked about. Main Street wasn't too busy for a Thursday morning and she prayed the shops were empty so her nosey conversation wouldn't be overheard. Only the banks had queues out front. Pension day, of course, they'd be busy.

Laurie stepped closer to her. "You can do this and you know it. Once you get started, you'll be fine. You might actually like it. We know you love to chat. This chat's just a little more focused than usual. Keep that mind."

She nodded, not surprised at his persuasiveness. No wonder his auction rates were good.

Laurie waved to a few guys across the street. "I know this is not what you expected, but sometimes when you're in business you have to do some ugly things to grow and this is one of those."

He continued. "Sometimes you've got to go into the fire to understand anything. You don't learn anything by standing around the edges looking in."

She turned to go inside. "I think I'll work on a little dialogue so I don't faff anything."

He beat her to the front door and blocked her entry. "Jen, truly, I know it's not easy, but think of it this way. After this exercise everyone around here will see you as the go-to girl for all things local with the locals. You'll know their needs. It beats them having to come up here and tell me. What's wrong with you being the face *Laurie Chester's Realty* dealing with local property?"

Stunned, words failed her. If only she could tape his words and play them back later. Too many bosses had let her down with promises. Was he hinting that he'd make her permanent, or was he selling her a piece of fluff to get her to do this door knock?

Jen stepped away from him and into the bright sunshine. She studied the street, a street she knew well, spotting Mrs M bustling down the street with Hannah chatting by her side, saw Reg head into the butchers and Edwina Lette having a laugh outside the bank.

What harm was there in staking a claim to a job? He wanted her to help build his business. Could she be so bold? Laurie could be an immovable object when it suited him.

She swallowed hard. "So you're going to make me permanent?"

He held up his hands and then shunted them straight into his pockets. "Now, now, now, don't get ahead of yourself there, Jen. I haven't forgotten it's up for discussion."

Jen bit back a sigh to hide her disappointment. No way did she want Laurie to get the idea she was desperate. No way did she want to spend the rest of her working life checking the fridge for fresh milk and putting the kettle on. If he could set himself on fire, so could she.

Jen looked him square in the eye before she forced her way past him, picked up her handbag from her desk, threw a couple of jelly beans in her side pocket, straightened her jacket and pulled her hair from her shoulders so it flowed down her back. On her way out she gave him a quick nod.

"Okay. I'll get going. See you later."

Chapter Sixteen

B rock cruised down Main Street looking for a car
space as close to Laurie's Realty as he could find. His
appointment to drop off the car and meet up with Laurie
didn't take place for another hour and coming in early gave
him the perfect excuse to get away from Gareth and have a
coffee somewhere.

His head still throbbed after a night of listening to his
brother's rantings. Not for the first time did he wonder
if madness ran through their family. He only knew his
father's family and had not a clue about his mother, or her
family.

Despite his brother's intelligence Brock felt sure a certain part of him often lost touch with reality. Gareth's
thoughts were getting dangerous and during the past week
he hadn't discussed any plans with Brock. His stomach
churned at that thought.

His brother's behaviour had often bordered on being obsessive and erratic, but since moving into Bindarra
Creek he could now add unpredictable and uncontrol-

lable. For him that meant frightening and he didn't know where things would end.

What was his brother planning? And what trouble would they be in? If the police got involved, he could kiss his future goodbye.

How had it gotten this far?

Brock turned up the air-con, anything to clear his mind and feel a little refreshed. He'd hardly slept since catching up with Jen in the private road. His brother's midnight rantings of what he'd done to Molly sickened him. He wondered how much Jen suspected. She wouldn't be easily fooled by his excuse of walking the back streets with Jasper.

The image of Jen's pale face, quivering lips and luminous eyes, with a tear trailing down one side of her face, would stay with him forever. He could live with a lot of things, but seeing her raw emotion tore at his gut.

What started out as an adventure had now morphed into something far more dangerous. He needed to keep a much closer eye on his brother.

A blonde head caught his attention. He eyed her as she stood in front of one shop and studied it, and then moved onto the next. What was Jen up to?

He did a quick u-turn and gave his horn a light tap. It's sound loud enough for Jen to turn around and see him. He wound down the window on the passenger side.

"Hiya, Jen."

She flicked him a glance and kept walking. His heart almost missed a beat. He hadn't figured her to be the type to hold a grudge. Then he saw it, the start of a smile.

"Come on, Jen. I can't cruise at this speed all day."

She kept walking and flicked him another glance.

"I don't respond to car horns."

He burst out laughing and drove on ahead. Three shop fronts down he spotted an empty car space close to Laurie's and parked the car.

Three minutes later he sauntered over to her where she stood feigning disinterest. Something about that cheered him.

As he walked towards her it struck him he didn't see any guile, no "come hither" fake glance, no sexy promise lacing her smile, just a lovely wide smile full of excitement and fun. He couldn't take his eyes off her and he slowed down to a saunter as he lapped up every nuance about her. She was dressed in a dark red skirt and white blouse, her long hair, blonde and swinging around her neck and shoulders unhindered.

He only knew one type of woman, the takers, but Jen tickled every nerve in his body.

He drew up in front of her and could smell a faint hint of apple blossom. "What do you respond to?"

She fluttered her eyelashes at him. "I'm not telling."

"There aren't too many people I honk a horn for." He had no idea what he was doing, but he didn't care. This was fun.

She looked up at him, her sweet expression unmissable, her cheeks flushed. "You don't have a choice, do you? I'm practically the only woman on this side of the street."

Words caught in his throat. *You're the only one I want to know.*

***

What is he doing? Is he playing games with me? Two can play at that. She needed to get a little more calculating when dealing with either of the Colder brothers.

Jen knew most of the young guys in town, all fit and active; none had such a powerful masculine presence as Brock Colder. It oozed out of every pour of his body. His stance, solid chest, and his unequalled air of confidence all drew her in. Any woman would lose her head over him.

He's out of my league.

She fought hard to temper her imagination. Her mind ran wild. Cheeky ideas, seriously sexy fun ideas, were taking root inside her head. The man was dangerous. She doubted she could ever look at him again without getting a flash of a seriously flirty idea.

He leaned in with a lazy smile. "You free for a coffee?"

"Coffee?"

His words brought her down to earth with a thud. Jen stared up at him, a relative newcomer in town, for what seemed the longest time and fought hard against her body's desire. Her wild amorous thoughts vanished to be replaced with random thoughts over the past few days.

"I'd love a coffee, but not right now. I'm working and I'll be tied up for quite a few hours. "

"I understand. Another time." Brock ran a hand through his hair. Now he looked boyish. Now her thoughts were stuck on the seriously cheeky idea circuit.

"I was cursing Laurie Chester to hell and back when you bipped your horn. He's got me doing a terrible job."

"What is it? You never know, he might give you a bonus."

Jen couldn't take her eyes off the man; his eyes were as warm and comforting as his voice when he laughed.

"You don't know Laurie. He's got me knocking on every shop in town asking what their future plans are. Are you leaving? Are you staying? If you're leaving, here's my card."

She groaned.

"Don't mind Laurie. He's in business. Learn from it." He laughed with the easy ready smile she liked. "Listen to me; you've got me sounding like a preacher."

His blue eyes turned serious and zeroed in on her.

She saw his hesitancy and leaned in a little closer, which wasn't that hard at all to do.

"What's your real problem?" he asked.

"I'm not permanent." Her words flew out as if she were playing ping pong with the man. Straight back at him and didn't hold back.

How did that happen? How could she do it? Reveal such a personal problem she'd been months trying to solve? It hurt that nobody in town wanted to make her a permanent member of their staff. It ate at her and now he knew it.

Brock didn't flinch or give her an ounce of sympathy.

"Oh, that's even easier. Think of yourself as a one-woman business. You're learning to deal with people, deal with whatever is happening with them right now – he's offering you the best lesson ever. Don't shy away from it. Play his game."

His silky smooth phrases were not exactly what she expected. She thought about his words. Jen never saw herself as a one woman business, except for her little side hustle of selling make-up at parties.

"Keep a second note-book; ask a few other questions and find out what's really going on in town and something else might be on offer for you. You might walk away with ideas, or, you might not. I'm just throwing that out there for you."

Jen took a surreptitious peek at him as he nodded to someone passing by. Things were colliding in her life and she could feel her mood shifting and lifting at all sorts of possibilities. It pained her to acknowledge it, but Laurie was right; she knew these people and they would speak to her. They saw her as harmless, good old Jen.

Nobody sees me as a threat.

That must also mean Brock and Gareth. She took a deep breath. "Brock, you mentioned needing a bookkeeper. Is that still on the table?"

His eyes widened. "It is. I'm no good with paper-work and Gareth is the salesman of the family. You interested?"

Jen shook her head. "No, not me, but Mel is. She's a bookkeeper. We thought she could do the books and I drop it off to you once a week on my way home? How does that sound?"

He grinned at her. "That works. I'll speak to Mel about it when I go in to see Laurie."

A thought struck her. "I don't get it. I thought Gareth was heading to Sydney. Why would you want to build up a business together if he's leaving?"

Brock pursed his lips. "Reg is looking to sell the garage and wants to build it up a little so the figures look good. We're on a six-month lease with him to do just that."

"How much longer on the lease to run?" she asked.

"Four months, we might break it earlier, who knows?"

His answer blew her away. *They've been in Bindarra Creek for two months?* She'd only been aware of their presence for a week. How was that even possible? Detail. Laurie is always harping on about the importance of detail, and how much it matters. While the town was asleep these guys were working on detail. Finding out heaven knows what kind of info. They had a plan, snuck into town, and decided when and how to make their presence known.

Laurie's right. You don't learn about anything until you ask the right question.

He's being honest with me, as if he had nothing to hide. She threw back her head and let out a gentle laugh. "I have to get going. Speak to Mel about the details. She'll do them, but I can easily drop them off to you on my way home from work. How does that work?"

"Perfect" Brock said before he sauntered away.

Jen stood and watched him until he entered The Cyprus Café. She loved his advice. The man was a mixed bag. Did she just pass up the perfect opportunity to get to know Brock better? If she'd have been any other woman, she'd have swung by Laurie and announced she'd be taking an early lunch and gone off with Brock. She wasn't another woman, she was Jennifer Rogers.

She glanced down Main Street. There were more people about and very few she didn't know.

Happy after her chat with Brock she pulled out her pen ready for some important conversations.

Chapter Seventeen

As Jen climbed out of her car after a long day at work, she took a deep breath of the sweet scent from a nearby bloom. She looked across at the McKenna homestead from their carpark, which ran down one side of the home. As usual it was lit up like a Christmas tree, with large, bright lights on every corner of the house and smaller ones nestled underneath the eaves. Taylah's mother believed a well-lit house said "you're welcome" to all her guests. Over the years, the girls - Hannah, Taylah and Jen - made fun of the "over the top" display at every opportunity.

Right now, Jen understood. She welcomed its warmth tonight as it had been a rough week. In fact it had been rough ever since the Colder brothers arrived on her doorstep.

She loved to be with her second family, to bunker down with them and chill out. Jen pulled out her make-up kit, slammed shut her car door and walked up the back steps.

Once inside, she followed the laughter and headed down the hall and walked into the kitchen. With soap suds up to her elbows Mrs McKenna – Mrs M, as Jen called her - stood at the kitchen sink while the evening news blared from the television in the corner; Taylah stood by her mother chatting and Hannah was hunched over her laptop at the dining room table.

Mrs M loved her charity shops and her kitchen and dining room were a testament to that love. Knick-knacks were everywhere and the three flying ducks above the stove made for a good conversation starter at many of Hannah's get-togethers for her horse-owners. The many jars along the back bench were filled with notes, pens and scissors, right down to the old-fashioned lace doilies which sat under empty vases and ornaments.

Jen waved her bag of goodies in the air. "You ready for your apple blossom and kiwi fruit scrub?"

On seeing Jen Mrs M quickly grabbed a towel and dried her hands. "I sure am. How are you, pet?"

Jen set down her bags next to Hannah. "Okay. You've heard about Molly then?"

Mrs M grimaced. "We have. Your dad's mentioned it a couple of times."

Hannah reached out and gave her hand a quick squeeze. "We loved Molly and her waddle."

"Oh yeah! I think everyone in town heard JoJo," said Taylah, picking up the kettle and filling it.

Jen strolled over to Taylah and leaned against the sink. "Guess where we found Molly and who was hanging around nearby?"

Taylah shook her head.

"Brock. Does one hundred and fifty ring a bell? Molly was left right under that letter box which has the numbering on it."

Taylah pulled down some coffee mugs. "So he's found the old homestead."

"Yes. It's right up there on the verge, you can't miss it. And we don't see it from our place, so we won't know if anybody's been checking anything out."

"Any alarms at the old homestead?"

Jen shook her head. "No, nobody goes there."

She headed straight for the back of her bag, brought out a packet of chocolate biscuits and plated them up. She kicked off her shoes and settled in the chair opposite Mrs M.

Taylah gave her a coffee and Jen looked across at Mrs M, a woman she'd known all her life, and someone who'd lived next door at the time of the robbery.

Jen played with her cup, turning it one way and then the other, unsure of how to start. All day long the questions kept popping in her head, but now at crunch time, her questions stalled in the back of her throat.

"What is it, pet?"

Jen grimaced. "Do you think anybody's found the stolen jewellery or the money?"

The room fell silent. Hannah jumped up and switched off the television. "That sounds more interesting than the news."

Mrs M shot Jen a quick look. "What's your dad saying?"

Jen shook her head. "Not much. That day is a closed shop. Do you remember JoJo before the robbery?"

Mrs M busied herself straightening a clean towel on the table.

"I sure do. She was petite with long thick blonde hair and she had the palest blue eyes. She and Stan got married and lived out at the old homestead caring for his grandmother when the old girl died. To everyone's surprise she left him some money."

Jen raised an eyebrow.

Mrs M nodded. "Enough to make a small deposit on a house, but they decided instead to go into business and opened the jewellery shop in town."

"Why jewellery?"

Mrs M rubbed her forehead. "They went to Tamworth for their honeymoon and decided to look for an engagement ring. They found a gem cutter who had a side business where he made rings and necklaces out of the stone off-cuts from other rings he'd made. I think they got the idea from him to sell the rings he designed."

Jen helped herself to a chocolate biscuit. "I can just remember JoJo's engagement ring because it was so different. It wasn't a diamond ring."

"The shop they opened was another outlet for this guy to sell his stuff. He sourced the off-cut stones and created the rings and necklaces. Stan made a monthly trip to purchase the next set of jewels. This guy was brilliant, a real artist. He'd fashion the setting to suit the shape of the stone, that's what made them unique. They stood out and were very modern for their time."

"Were they doing okay?"

Mrs M sat back. "I think so. They were selling one-off unique pieces, no two were the same. All the pieces varied in shape, size, and depth of colour, and your uncle Stan used that as a unique selling point. From the get-go I think Stan saw it was a business opportunity and it worked."

"Did you ever buy a ring from them?"

Mrs M shook her head. "Like a lot of women around here, I was saving up for one. I'm sorry I didn't put one on layby, that's what you did then."

Jen nodded, but she needed to really get a clear picture in her head. "Sort of. A picture's forming. Do you remember much about the robbery? Do you remember that day?"

Mrs M smiled. "I was here, at home, that day. I've heard that three guys walked into the shop, got into the display cabinets and tipped the trays of rings and bracelets into some bags. They pushed JoJo around at first, being in the shop, but when Stan came out from the back room, they bashed him senseless. Well, you know how that ended. JoJo never recovered."

"Weren't the display cases locked?" persisted Jen.

"I couldn't tell you, pet. Probably only some, I don't think anybody did in those days. We didn't have a lot of robberies then. It was a different time."

Jen rubbed her forehead. She swore her head ached from over-thinking. Something didn't work in Mrs M's story.

A phone buzzed. Hannah pulled out her phone. "A fox is in the stables. I've got to go. I won't be long."

Jen offered her a chocolate biscuit from the plate as she passed by, which Hannah picked up as she strode out of the dining room.

"But, didn't anybody come in to help?"

"Not until JoJo ran out and screamed. There weren't too many people on the street and I don't think they had an alarm. Even if they did I don't know if JoJo would have thought to use it."

Jen slumped deeper in her chair. "Thanks, you've plugged a few story holes for me. Dad's a bit of a brick wall sometimes."

Mrs M's raised an eyebrow and Jen took the hint. "Talking about brick walls, isn't it time for your masque? You ready?"

Without another word Jen jumped up and opened a beautiful new jar of the latest apple blossom and kiwi fruit scrub.

Two hours later Jen stood in the doorway of her father's shed. She watched him as he sat on an old rusty pull-out chair and read a brown dog-eared newspaper clipping. This new habit of her father's to come out here of an evening worried her mother. Curious now, Jen stepped further inside the shed. Her father didn't notice.

Around his feet were numerous brown and dusty boxes, boxes she'd never seen.

Behind him lined up against the back wall were the familiar grey boxes which housed his memorabilia, including ribbons and paper clippings, covering his early racing career as a top country jockey.

She knocked on the door. "What are you looking at, Dad?"

Her father's head lifted and a rush of tenderness rippled across his face. "Hello there. How's my favourite girl?"

"Good. It's been a rough time lately.' She walked over to the side wall and picked up her father's pull-out chair's mate, just as she had the previous time. Once opened, she flopped in it and sat opposite him.

She picked out some clippings from the nearest box. "What are you doing out here?"

He shot her a careful glance. "Did your mother send you?"

She shook her head. She saw the headlines "Jewellery Store Robbery", "Man attacked in robbery".

"Dad, what are you looking for? What are you up to?"

He started to tidy up the assortment of papers and photos around his feet.

He kicked a few of the boxes to make some space.

"What were you looking for?"

Her father let out a gruff cough. "Nothing in particular. I just wanted to refresh my memory about that time."

She pounced. "Mrs M said tonight that Uncle Stan sold unique jewellery pieces. Did you ever buy any for Mum?"

Her father almost choked on a laugh. "No, love. Not at his prices. They were way out of my reach, but I always fancied buying one for your mother one day. That day's just never happened."

She edged closer to her father.

"Do you know where they are now?"

Her father stared at her for the longest time. "One was killed in a car accident on his way to Sydney a day or two later, and the other was killed years later in a drunken fight at Broken Hill."

"And the other?"

Her father waved his arms about. "He disappeared into thin air. Nobody's heard a word from him, not the army, his bank, nothing. How do you do that?" Her father shrugged as he stood up to pack away his chair.

She did likewise, but her mind wouldn't rest. "What was his name?"

"Alan Colt."

Jen dropped her head. "Dad," she whispered. "There are two new guys in town and their surname is Colder. I think Alan Colt changed his name to Colder."

Her father started.

Jen laid a hand on his knee. "I've mentioned it to Abby, she's aware of the connection and she was going to speak to them."

Her father let out a soft sigh. He seemed to age in those few minutes. "Thanks, pet. So he changed his name. Now you mention it, that's the obvious thing to do. At least the police know."

She reached across and kissed her father's forehead. "Don't you worry. I'll keep on top of it."

Chapter Eighteen

The following morning Jen drove back to the McKenna's place before she left for work. From their carpark she could see her father riding and Hannah standing at the barriers. Her father was the last rider on the track and Jen knew they were almost finished training.

"You timed this well," called out Mrs M as she carried a tray of bacon butties to the shed next to the stables.

Jen took a deep breath. "I can smell them from here. You got a spare one for me?"

"Always."

Jen joined Mrs M and together they walked towards Hannah but waited until she'd finished.

After a few minutes Hannah shut down her tablet where she recorded on charts each horse's progress. She waved to Jen. Her long hair flowed down her back and she was dressed in her work clothes, jeans and a t-shirt worn with thick woollen socks tucked into her Wellington gumboots, Hannah lived for her horses.

"Morning Jen, you're the just one I need. Are you free on Sunday morning? I need another track rider."

Jen rubbed her hands. "Sure, not a prob, but, I do have a favour to ask both of you and it's a pretty big one."

Hannah joined her on the bench. "This sounds serious. Whatever it is, I say yes. What is it?"

"Well, this all started with me wanting to give Mum a break for a couple of hours a week. They have child-care centres for children, but there's nothing here for carers to have a break from the people they care for. I thought if we had a backyard and a room at either the Council or the hospital with some trained nurses to care for patients like JoJo, it would free carers like Mum to do a bit of shopping without..."

"JoJo's drama," finished Hannah.

"That's it."

"And?" encouraged Hannah.

"As a fund raiser to pay for furniture, assistance and anything we need, my idea was to sell tickets for a first dates dinner party. I was thinking about having it here. You have the biggest verandah I know with the best view."

Mrs M reached out and gave her hand a squeeze. "Of course, pet, we can fit ten or more out there. You give me a date and it's on."

Jen hugged Mrs M. "Thank you. I'll do as much as I can. Thank you."

Hannah sat back in her chair and grinned across at Jen. "Sounds good, but you have one major problem."

She let Mrs M go. "What?"

"You'll have all the singles in town buying tickets, but what about everyone else? I'm sure lots of people would want to get behind it and buy tickets. You'll have to offer other prizes."

"I thought of that. I was going to offer monthly facials for a year for men or women. What do you think?"

Mrs M burst out laughing. "I was going to say I can't see too many guys buying into that, but with these modern guys I could wrong. A monthly facial would go down well."

Hannah wound her hair into a bun. "I think it sounds great. Better still, mention it on Sunday morning when everyone's here and in my weekly blog I'll post a mention."

"What date were you looking at?"

"The last Saturday night in October."

Mrs M gave her the thumbs up. "We'd better start working on a menu."

Jen leaned across and grabbed a bacon buttie. "I totally forgot about that."

Mrs M grabbed the tray. "I'll take this down to your father and Taylah. I'm sure they're starving."

Chapter Nineteen

On the following Sunday morning at the McKenna's preparations were underway for Hannah's monthly Q&A get together with her clients and potential clients to showcase her horses. From the verandah, Jen searched the crowd for some familiar faces. She could see her plan going pear-shaped if the bulk of the crowd were from Sydney. How many Sydney-siders would drive to Bindarra Creek for a first date's dinner?

Standing opposite her, at the top corner of the carpark, was Jen's mother under the shade of a large umbrella offering cold drinks. Beside her a happy JoJo smiled as she handed out today's program to the guests. A slow trickle of visitors walked past them on their way to the make-shift stage and seating area in front of the race track.

Hannah had spent a small fortune on establishing a hedge alongside the path that led to the race track, with a small rose garden at either end. Pity it's the wrong season to flower, thought Jen. Fingers crossed the kangaroos don't eat the rose buds next winter.

With a ten am start she had thirty minutes left to get her head into gear.

From the McKenna verandah she watched as their carpark filled up, with the odd local giving her a wave. She'd only ever seen it so full at Hannah's annual Christmas party. Jen's hand shook as she clutched her notes every time she saw another car drive up.

Jen turned to Hannah who sat at a small table on the verandah. "Hannah, can't you make a public announcement about the first dates auction before you start today's session? Just slip in a few extra words, that should do it."

"Sorry Jen, no can do. This auction is your baby," said Hannah as she checked the updated charts of each horse.

Jen never missed Hannah's Q&A session every month. She loved being part of it, especially when she rode the horses down the straight as Hannah introduced them on stage. A year ago Hannah had introduced the monthly sessions to show her thoroughbred horses to her clients and interested parties. Now she showcased not only her own horses but a few from some local breeders. Each month it grew and today was by far the largest crowd to attend.

"Hannah, who did you invite? There's only a few here I know."

Hannah grinned as she packed up her laptop before heading to the stables. "It works every time. I sent out a newsletter and people ticked the 'yes' box to attend. I never think newsletters work, but they do."

She leaned across and snatched Jen's notes from her hands. "You don't need these. Speak from the heart; people will love it."

Jen groaned. "No, no, no."

Hannah gave her a quick hug. "Yes, yes, yes. People like to see vulnerability; they like to see raw honesty. They'll love you for it."

With a cheeky grin, Hannah made a show of folding Jen's notes and putting them in the back pocket of her jeans. "You'll thank me for it later." She waved goodbye, and then left her to meet and greet her guests.

One by one more cars arrived. Jen spotted Taylah running up from the stables to start directing people to park along the back paddock and walk up the driveway.

Make yourself useful.

She ran down the driveway, past Taylah, and indicated she'd go to the gate. She kept her eye on the dirt track, careful to miss the pot holes. On her way down a car horn pipped. Jen waved to Laurie and Mel, who never missed a session. Laurie rarely left the office, but enjoyed Hannah's sessions. Jen suspected he did his own meet and greet on these days.

"Hi Jen, good to see you."

Jen looked up and saw Blake Hudson, Hannah's husband cruise by. He lived a few days in Sydney and the half part of the week working with Hannah. She waved back at him.

Jen stood in the sun, beside the wooden post near the *Blue Orchard Park* sign. The entry gate to the McKenna property was at the lower end of their property, a dry, treeless and airless patch of dirt. Jen was hot, sticky and dusty. After a few minutes a trickle of sweat started to run down her back. It tickled.

Jen waved at each new driver, pointing to where Taylah stood at the crest of the hill. As a car drove past she went too far backward and her sunglasses fell down the back of her head. She fumbled picking them up. Each time her moist fingers touched them, they tumbled in the air. On the fourth attempt she nabbed them.

"Fumble fingers. How are you, Jennifer Rogers?"

Jen straightened. Gareth and Brock Colder sat in a black SUV looking fresh and cool. The Sydney girls here will love them, mused Jen. Both of them looked too hot to touch, let alone handle.

Forget that. They were with her now.

She stepped closer.

Gareth, who sat at the driver's wheel, inclined his head. "Jen, thanks for organising Mel to do our books."

"My pleasure."

Gareth pointed to the property "Where do you want us to go?"

Jen stepped back. "Oh, sorry. Yes, of course. Straight up and veer right. I'm afraid you'll have to park on the grass verge. We're busier than normal today. You'll see the track from the carpark and just head on down."

Stop blabbering.

Both men waved as they went by. As the last of the cars drove past she headed up the small incline. When she hit the carpark she spotted the brothers reaching the race track. They wove their way around searching for an empty seat.

Both men turned heads. Brock moved well as he navigated his way through the milling crowd. Dressed in a dark blue cotton shirt it clung to every sculptured muscle on his chest and back. In contrast, Gareth wore a pale blue shirt, contrasting with tanned face, he too was hard to miss.

Taylah joined her and followed her line of sight. "I think they're both going to need body-guards."

Jen looked away from the handsome brothers. "It won't last. They're a novelty right now."

They saw Hannah step onto the stage. Jen let out a few nervous breaths as she walked down the uneven grass verge toward the stage.

"Good morning, everyone. Welcome to *Blue Orchard Park*. For those of you who don't know me, I'm Hannah McKenna and it's lovely to see so many people here. Before we begin today, I have somebody who'd like to talk to you about something very close to her heart. You'll see her riding some of our beautiful horses today. Please welcome Jennifer Rogers."

The crowd hollered and clapped.

Despite her fear, Jen's lips moved in the direction of a smile. She couldn't help it; the crowd's enthusiastic response caught her off-guard. Maybe there were more locals here than she thought. She'd grown up in this town, they all knew her family well, and if she ever left, she'd always come back and call it home.

With what seemed to be a hundred sets of eyes on her, Jen kept her eyes anchored on Hannah, who gave her encouraging nods as she made her way to the stage. The clapping slowed down; she took a very long deep breath and grabbed the mic.

"Hello, everybody. I have a few questions for the singles out there. Who likes to date? Who likes a surprise?"

More loud clapping. That worked.

Her gaze snagged on Brock. The man is a total distraction.

"I'm up here to talk about a cause that is very close to our hearts - carers. These unseen, beautiful people give up so much to care for a loved one. We have a lot of carers in our community. To care full time for somebody you sacrifice a lot. Some people give up their jobs, their lifestyle and enter another world. It's selfless work; it's exhausting and its twenty-four hours, seven days a week. In Bindarra Creek we'd like to give our carers a break. We're raising funds to provide a safe place with a professional carer, to look after family members."

Brock gave her encouraging nods.

"Now for the fun stuff. We're holding a first dates auction."

The crowd broke out into cheers and claps. Jen let out a breath and looked down at Hannah, who gave her the thumbs up.

"There will be twelve tickets to win and the McKenna family has kindly offered to host the dinner which will be on the last night in October. It will take place here and besides having a lovely meal, you'll be overlooking some beautiful countryside. "

Laurie stood up and turned to the crowd. "Three cheers for the McKenna family. Hip hip!"

"Hooray!" The crowd let loose with their cheers. Laurie turned to her and clapped.

"Hip Hip!" He pumped his fisted above his head, revving the crowd. Their cheer grew louder.

"Hip hip!" Laurie shouted.

"Hooray!"

Hannah stood up and clapped the crowd. She mouthed "thank you", but nobody heard her over the laughter.

Jen shook her head. "Thanks, Laurie. From where I'm standing, it looks to me like you're in the mood to spend some money. Keep that thought. Remember the lady who handed out the drinks when you arrived? She's my mother, Pam. She's a carer and is selling the tickets. If you love to date and love a surprise this is the deal for you. Tickets are one hundred dollars each. For the romantics in you, please don't sell yourself short. Get yourself a ticket to a fun night. On Saturday night, the twenty-second of October at six o'clock, we'll announce the twelve winners at the

Riverside pub. Now, enough from me. I'll hand you back to Hannah and I'll head for the stables. Thank you!"

Hannah grinned at Jen as she joined her on stage. "That was brilliant. What did I tell you? The heart speaks! I should get you up here more often."

Jen handed her back the mic. "It's all yours."

"Just one minute, folks, one more minute." Gareth strode toward them on the stage. He put his hand out. "Hannah, may I?"

She nodded.

The crowd hushed, all eyes were on him.

Gareth waved to the crowd, as if he'd been born to the stage. "I'm Gareth Colder and my brother, Brock, is sitting over there in the third row. We're new to town and plan to buy five tickets each to try and get a place at that table. We'd love to meet some locals and I'm up here to ask you all to dig deep."

Five tickets each blew Jen's mind. Her mother clasped her hand over her mouth. The crowd clapped and two girls in the back row stood up and wolf whistled.

At the corner of her eye Jen saw her father. His eyes were on Brock and she watched as he walked down the right hand side of the seats, same side as Brock. When he reached Brock's row he stared at him, his face an unreadable mask.

Gareth turned to Jen, his face beaming at her. "Hope it helps, Jen."

Stunned, Jen nodded and followed him off the stage. Gareth touched her arm. "I forgot to mention, about the books. Mel said you were okay with dropping off the profit & loss statements to us. Want to start next Saturday afternoon? Does that work for you?"

Jen grinned at him. "Of course. I'll drop it in on my way home from work. Thanks, Gareth."

He waved her on. "Good, see you then."

Without glancing at anybody she headed straight for the stables. Hannah's latest horse, Lady Dancer, was first up.

"Hey, Jen. Hold up for a minute will you?"

Brock. Her feet had their own rules and they stopped mid-stride. "Brock, I'm sorry, I'm first up." Still her feet remained in position and she pivoted her body to face him.

He caught up and tapped her lightly on the back.

"I don't want to hold you up. Quick question, will you be buying tickets yourself? Or just overseeing?"

What's he saying here? A tick of pleasure shot through her.

She shrugged. "No. I'll be helping out. Probably doing the dishes."

Brock stepped closer. So close she could see the flecks in his blue eyes. "I'm happy to help out on the night. I can do dishes." He ran a hand across his face. "I can't believe I just said that. Call me if you need a hand on the night."

"You might win a ticket."

"I might not, too. Anything I can do at all to help for the auction?"

Jen thought about that. What could he do? She grinned at him. "I know. Could you please make up a big sign when the winners are announced? Something with the date, address and location of the dinner?"

Brock grinned at her. "Easy done. You go. I'll catch you later."

Jen grabbed his hand. "Come on down and meet everyone." Together they walked the rest of the way down the narrow path that led to the stables. When they reached the stables her father stood in the doorway, his expression unreadable.

"Dad, I'd like you to meet Brock Colder. Come on, Taylah, don't be shy."

Taylah stood at the other end of the stable carrying a saddle. Taylah nodded. "Nice to meet you, Brock. If you'll excuse me."

He waved to her.

Brock turned to her father and held out his hand. "Nice to meet you, Mr Rogers."

Her father held up a pair of greasy hands. "Nice to meet you, Brock. Sorry, but you've got me on a busy day. I've been rubbing down one of the horses."

Brock nodded to her father. "All good. I'll head off." He turned to Jen, "I'll catch you later."

In another blink he was gone.

"What did handsome want?" He father asked.

"If you must know, he offered to prepare a sign about it and do the dishes on the night of the first dates' dinner."

Her father raised an eyebrow. "Well, that's a new pick-up line."

"Dad, it's no pick-up line. He's looking for ways to get involved in the community."

Her father strode to the wall opposite her and pulled down a saddle. "They're like their father, big, blond and brazen. They're opportunists just like their father. I don't trust either of them. There's something not right about the pair of them."

Jen followed her father. "Dad, you're looking at this the wrong way."

He turned, his eyes blazing. "Somebody ought to be looking out for Reg. He's got those beautiful cars and these guys have just waltzed into town, got Reg to agree to lease them his garage which has been closed for ten plus years at least. They're here for the jewels and money. I don't know what else would bring them to town. Anyway I've spoken to Abby about it. She's looking into it. It's a cold case. "

Chapter Twenty

The following Saturday afternoon Jen headed for the garage. Maybe this was a bad idea. As she drove across Kingfisher Bridge she stared in amazement at the number of motor bikes parked on the grass verge which ran alongside the highway. Usually cars were parked like this on the opposite side of the road for a huge gig at the Riverside. Never ever this side of the bridge.

As she neared the entry, at least fifteen motor bikes were in front of the garage. Further along, she saw bikes parked down the side of the building, alongside Reg's old cars.

With no place to park, she did a u-turn, drove a little way and then did a second u-turn and double-parked as close as she could to the driveway leading to the garage.

What was going on? Did they get a big job and trailer loads of bikes were unloaded? Her brain could not compute how an almost desolate garage, could be so full.

Why?

She stared at the profit & loss statement Mel'd prepared for Gareth. *A promise is a promise*. If he wasn't in, she'd stuff it under the door.

As she climbed out of her car, she heard a loud hum, then silence. She walked half-way down the driveway and turned back. She stared at the building and bikes. Something about the place seemed off.

You've come all this way.

She gave a nervous glance at the main garage, and did an about turn and marched straight to the smaller office and stuffed the profit & loss statement under the door. She'd text Gareth where to find it.

At that moment the garage door burst open and two young guys, dressed in leather pants and black t-shirts, fell out onto the dirt, grappling one another as they rolled in the dust. A can of beer shot across the dirt path.

She froze. The double open door gave her a bird's eye view of about thirty guys standing in a large circle. The garage was cloudy from smoke; she could smell it, thick, choking and foul.

"I didn't know you brought entertainment, guys," someone yelled.

His words woke her, jerked her back to reality. Jen took a step backward.

All eyes turned to her and fear gripped her like she'd never known before. She fought hard to stay upright as she stared into the garage. The two guys fighting bare-knuckle in the circle kept on fighting, unaware the cheers and jeers had stopped.

"Oh, no you don't, darling. What were you doing out here?" She didn't know the owner of those words, but her eyes were drawn to one figure.

Sitting on a chair on the back bench straight ahead of her sat Gareth with a cigar in one hand, a stopwatch and chain swinging from the other, and a black back-pack swinging around one of his shoulders.

"Good god, look who's just walked in," boomed Gareth. He stood up, clenched his fists and then flung his arms up above his head. In an instant the soft chatter ceased and the two guys stopped fighting. They looked up at Gareth, who'd stopped orchestrating their fight. By his side were two guys taking bets, small notebooks and pens in hand, with bags of cash around their waist.

"What are you doing here, Jen?" he repeated.

All eyes turned to her and she shivered. Some eyes were red as if they hadn't slept in days, others had an excited glaze about them, and those on the fringes had a crazy expression shifting in their eyes, while some of their bodies listed from side to side.

She swallowed down her fear. "I've brought in the profit & loss statement I promised. I've left it under the doorway next door." Her words spilled over. "I'm sorry."

A scrawny guy close to the open door leaned up and scratched his head. "Well fancy that; you're the only person I know who keeps promises."

The room burst out into raucous laughter.

A pain hot and sharp shot through her chest. *Is that a heart attack?* Her arms were too stiff to move to rub her chest. She tried to breathe, but all she could manage were little puffs.

A tall figure came out of the shadows from behind Gareth. Brock shoved guys to his left and right as he walked the length of the garage. Nobody touched him as he pushed his way through the men toward her. His face, expressionless.

The two guys who were outside with her rose to their feet and scrambled back inside.

As he cleared the doorway, he shot his hand out in front, for only her eyes, indicating she stay. Seeing him released a little of her fear, her breathing not so shallow.

Brock turned to the men. "My woman. I'll take care of business. I'll see her out."

With one almighty heave Brock kicked shut one of the double wooden doors. He strode to the other side to kick it closed when one of the older guys slipped out between the doors. He leered at her, his sick expression enhanced by the tattoos over his hairless skull, neck and every other piece of skin Jen could see, apart from his face.

He stepped closer to her. His toothless smile sent chills down her spine. "I want to see this. I'm checking to see if this is legit. You're not the usual type Brock goes for. This should be interesting," he declared.

Brock ignored the guy as he strode toward her. Her eyes followed him, her eyes devoured his every reassuring move until he stood in front of her. Only then did she release her breath. His face broke out into a warm smile as he put his arm about her shoulders.

"Come on, let's see you off. Where did you park?"

She couldn't speak, but grabbed him with one hand at his back, and clutched his shirt with the other at his front. She needed all his strength if she wanted to turn around and walk out. His warm hand massaged the back of her neck, with soft firm strokes. At his touch her body started to relax.

He held her close, his thigh whisper-touched hers as he guided her, in a very casual way, to turn around and walk the short path to the highway. Her stiff body complied. "Take a deep breath, come on now. In. Out. In. Out."

After a beat her body warmed as they walked toward her car. She was very aware of his hand on her neck and when it travelled down to her upper arm as he kept her upright.

"Keys, Jen. Where are your car keys?"

Her eyes darted to the passenger seat of the car and there sat her handbag. The door was locked. She opened her hand. Therein lay her keys.

Without a word, Brock gently prized the keys out of her hand.

Concern etched on his face as he looked into her eyes. "Will you be okay to drive home?"

She nodded. She wanted to be free of this place.

Brock's blue eyes deepened as he ran a hand down the side of her face. "We have to put on a show, a damn good show."

"A show?" she whispered.

In seconds he leaned close to her, so close her breasts crushed against his solid wall of chest. He bent his head, and then his lips hummed across hers with the lightest of touches. The intimate touch startled her, his gentle lips touching, urging hers to open, set off a lovely chain of yearning throughout her body. Jen reached out, wrapped her arms about his neck and pulled him ever closer to her. His long arms spiralled their way around her back as his kiss deepened, his tongue exploring her mouth.

Her fear fell away. Her heart rate shot up to a ridiculous beat. A surge of lust grew within her, cell by delicious cell.

Chapter Twenty-One

B rock pulled back, breaking the connection of their kiss. He closed his eyes and sucked in the air, the soft apple blossom scent wafting around Jen's hair. He wanted to tug loose her pony tail, to sink his face in her hair and breathe. Just to breathe in all her sweetness which made him feel so damn good.

His hands moved up to her shoulders in the hope of containing her slight tremors which matched his own. She sighed, a sigh filled with longing. It pained him to hear it, but he loved it. With great reluctance he lifted his head. Her beautiful green eyes rose to meet his. Her long lashes did nothing to hide the confusion in her eyes. He understood.

Her face released a slight blush, a soft hue of pink. He caught her hand as she reached up to touch him and squeezed it tight. For a while he refused to move. For the first time ever he wanted to keep the moment.

"You okay?" he asked shakily.

Jen gave him a shy smile. "I think so. A little surprised."

A short, sharp laugh nearby brought him to his senses.

Jen moved and he watched as she slowly slid her hand out from his. "I should go. It looked like you were busy in there."

And there ended the dream.

How had the gods construed it that he'd just kissed the loveliest girl he'd met? Jennifer Rogers didn't have a mean, shifty, malicious bone in her body. She was all goodness. How did it happen?

She would never be part of his world.

Without another word, he opened her car door and ushered her in.

She glanced up at him, her bottom lip trembling. "See you about."

He coughed; something about seeing her go didn't sit well. "Will you be okay to drive home?"

Brock's body felt charged with a rare energy. He wanted to roar, long and loud, into the air. Instead, he contained his feelings. He fisted his hands and shoved them in his pockets.

He slapped Jen's car, urging her to go home. He studied her messed pony tail as it wobbled about her head, the soft blonde curls at the nape of her neck, the pale pink polish on her nails and every part of him ached. He longed to join her, to take off and just leave.

He shouldn't think those thoughts. He had no right.

Jen represented so many lovely things that were so out of his reach. She belonged to a nice solid world. He was drawn to her sweetness and there was something inherently good in her. She was so not for him.

His past, his life with his family, dictated his future. She would never understand and had only glimpsed a bit of his world today.

His heart ached for her. He couldn't imagine what she thought or felt. He'd seen too much, heard too much and lived in a world she didn't understand or even know about. Today she'd glimpsed a little of his hell.

He boxed away the shock, the slight trace of lust and confusion in her eyes. He knew he mirrored those feelings. Damn.

How had it come to this? His total acceptance of and compliance with the business in the garage was wrong on so many fronts. It sickened him. His own participation disgusted him.

A powerful urge ripped through him to roar into that garage and kick everyone out. It frightened the hell out of him. Disappointment and anger swirled about him. He kept watch until her car disappeared from view. The slime ball who'd followed them slunk back into the garage. Half the garage door stood open and he saw King Gareth atop his throne orchestrating yet another fight. He'd seen many of these gatherings over the years.

He saw it with fresh eyes. How would she ever get rid of the raw image of a bare-knuckle fight? It was tough and brutal.

He knew Gareth wouldn't rest until the jewels and money were found, but she'd been a witness to this fight, to this depravity she probably never knew existed.

What type of a guy am I?

He let out a sigh and kicked at the loose stones on the pavement. Agitated, he paced the front yard, his thoughts slowly taking shape. She needed protection. He could watch over her.

What if she liked him? She'd responded to his kiss in a way that both shocked and delighted him. Could he see himself with someone like her?

Forget it. She was too good for him. All he could do now was to look out for her.

Chapter Twenty-Two

A few days later, Jen paced the outside undercover foyer of the Riverside. She was dressed in a pair of white jeans and her latest white top, which she loved for its three-quarter lacey sleeves and asymmetric hem, together with a pair of white strappy sandals. The place was fast filling up and permission had been given for Taylah to sit in the back corner and sell tickets. Luckily, people were still buying tickets.

But, she was missing one thing. Brock. He'd promised to bring along a sign showing the details of date, place and time for the dinner party. Maybe he forgot, it was only mentioned in passing.

Hannah walked in with her husband, Blake. Jen rarely saw Hannah out of jeans but tonight she wore a slinky black number with a split down one side. She looked gorgeous.

"Jen, have you the nervous jitters, or are you waiting for someone?"

"He's coming. Soon."

Hannah raised an eyebrow. "A date?"

Blake grinned as he steered Hannah toward the door. "Don't mind her, she's nosey. We'll see you inside."

Jen continued her pacing. She'd promised to help Brock in with the signs. She would keep the faith.

"Sweetheart, what are you doing out here?" Her mother rushed up to her and straightened her hair.

"Waiting for Brock, he's bringing the big sign. Don't mind me, Mum. He won't be long." She opened the door for her mother and watched her go inside.

Jen turned, and there he was standing on the edge of the carport. He'd dressed for the occasion and looked elegant in a dark suit, an edgy expression, and dangerous eyes. The guy packed a punch in every day clothes, but this was in another stratosphere.

Jen marshalled all the strength she had not to say something stupid. "Hi."

The expression on his face never changed from cool and calm. He walked over to her. "Hi." He took her hand and led her to the back of the building. "Sorry, I wanted to say something before we went inside and got caught up with everything."

Craning her neck, she stared up at him.

His eyes softened, they turned a deeper blue. "About that kiss."

The one that made my week, my day, set me on fire? The one I want repeated, over and over again?

Brock frowned.

Her heart quaked. *Oh, no, he's going to apologise.*

"I'm sorry it wasn't under nicer circumstances."

Jen let out a sigh.

He swallowed hard and she held her breath, waiting.

"There you are!" claimed Taylah as she grabbed Jen's arm. "Sorry, Brock it's all about to start."

Something flickered in his eyes, but he went back to his earlier cool, calm expression. That must be his coping mechanism; that cool, calm exterior hid a lovely soul. What did he want to say? Confession time? She wasn't sure, but it mattered and the moment had passed.

"Jen, are you out here?" asked Florrie.

"We're here," called out Brock. "I've got the sign. I'll bring it in."

"Okay," said Taylah. "Come on, Florrie we don't want to lose our seats."

"I'll help you with the sign," Jen offered and rushed after him.

In two shakes he'd lifted the sign out of his ute and carried it under one arm. He grinned at her. "All good."

He glanced about, saw they were alone and bent down to her and grazed his lips over hers. He kissed her cheek and whispered, "You look sensational."

Sensational.

Right there and then she swore if they were the last words she ever heard she'd be happy.

He put down the sign. "What do you think?"

She blinked twice. Jen imagined a simple sign saying "*First Dates' Dinner*" and the date and time. Her imagination was sadly lacking as she stared at the cheeky sign Brock had created. The wording stood out inside one big red heart, while outside that circle were a mix of broken hearts and solid hearts. Simple, but it made her smile.

"I love it."

Inside, she made her way to her family's table.

A mic screeched and on the stage stood Florrie Miller. Beside her was a small table and on that sat Jen's jelly-bean bowl from work, almost full to the brim with tickets. "No, no, Jen. You're headed in the wrong direction. Come on up here and tell us a little about what's been happening before I announce the winners. That's what we're all waiting on."

Jen blushed as all eyes turned on them. All eyes were on *them*.

She crisscrossed her way through the tables to the stage and managed to smile whenever someone caught her attention. She couldn't help but notice eyes drifted from her to Brock right behind.

Then she felt his big, warm hand at the small of her back guiding her. He was close, she felt his warmth, his ginger citrusy scent.

Which she loved, and wanted more of, so she took in another deep breath.

As they approached the stage she turned to him. "You can just drop off the sign." His answer was to nudge her up the stairs and onto the stage.

With a room full of eyes on her, she took the mic from Florrie who helped Brock set up the sign before they walked to the left of the stage and stood in the wings. Alone on stage, she never realised how big it was. Huge.

Jen took a few big deep breaths. "Good evening, Bindarra Creek."

The crowd went wild cheering and roaring.

Her fear fell away; their reaction both thrilled and excited her. She hadn't expected such enthusiasm. There weren't too many people in the room she didn't know, she'd either grown up with them or worked with them. There was an irreplaceable bond between them all. She realised that bond formed an integral part of her life that she took for granted. Seeing everyone behind her tonight meant the world to her.

"I can't believe what I'm seeing tonight. We've all dressed to impress. I can't see a ripped pair of jeans or a t-shirt anywhere in sight."

Again she was met with a wild roar from the crowd.

"Who's your boyfriend?"

This from Mel, with the cheekiest smile on her face, sitting beside Laurie at the front table.

Jen pretended she didn't hear.

"Come on, Jen. Who's your date?"

Jen's grip tightened on the mic. Her eyes shot to her mother, who looked miffed. "He's not my boyfriend. I've come here with family and friends. Can't a girl have a male friend?"

Everybody in town new her love life was woeful. Mel loved to stir. The laughter continued.

Jen could feel her face burn with embarrassment. Above the heat and noise Jen could not make out who were doing the call-outs.

"Who's your hot assistant then? We missed the intros."

She turned to the side of the stage and caught Brock checking her out. Instantly, her heart gave one solid pound. She saw the desire in his eyes. In that second her body heated and her thoughts scattered. Nothing mattered. Not her family, not work, not one damn thing. Nothing else mattered, except that really decent guy to her left.

On queue that really decent guy strode out from the wings to join her.

She could feel a change in the audience, the curiosity and the anticipation. Some of the ladies in the back were standing and vying for better viewing.

With great reluctance, she tore her eyes away from him and faced the audience. "You nosey lot should get a life."

Everyone laughed.

All eyes were on her so-called her hot assistant and Jen knew they couldn't start until she introduced him. She glanced up at him and knew. She really liked Brock Colder.

He leaned in closer to her, his arms and chest touching her shoulder. "Hi everyone," he addressed the crowd, his deep raspy voice silencing them. "Jen's being a little bashful. I'm Brock Colder, her date."

He slid her a hot bad-boy look, and her insides quivered.

She took the mic from him. "Now you know, let's get down to business. Bindarra Creek, you're wonderful! Thank you."

She took a step back. The crowd stood up and gave a long, loud cheer.

Jen waved her arm down in an effort to quieten them.

She gave them a huge smile. "We've had a fabulous response. It's been overwhelming and we've made a slight change. We decided to offer a second prize. It's for twenty people to be held at the same date, time and place as the first dates' dinner, but it will be a picnic barbeque on the grounds of *Blue Orchard Park*. I'd like to thank the McKenna family again for their extra generosity. Please give them a huge cheer."

Again, the crowd went wild.

Jen looked to the wings, and held out her arm. Florrie Miller walked out on stage.

"I'll hand the official part over to Florrie who will dip her hand in the bowl and name the lucky winners. Thank you!"

She quickly handed the mic over to Florrie, happy to leave the spot-light.

Brock tapped her on the shoulder. "Gareth's just down the back there. I'll catch you later."

Jen watched him walk past her and kept watch as he threaded his way through the crowd. A hand shot up and waved. Gareth. She gave him a curt nod.

"Colder," admonished her mother. "That boy looks a lot like his father, Alan *Colt*. There's bad blood in that family."

Jen sat on the chair beside her mother. "So, Dad told you."

Her mother nodded.

"Mum, I'm not a child."

Her mother handed her a cold drink. "Did you buy a ticket or two for the dinner? This place is full tonight, there's plenty of single guys out there from nice families."

"No, I didn't buy a ticket. I'll be helping out, serving and a heap of other things."

A light tap on her shoulder and she looked up at Mrs M. "Oh, pet. It's going to be fabulous. I didn't know we had so many singles in town. I'm all excited now."

"A Colt, now a Colder." Jen's mother shook her head, and would not leave the subject. "My girl walked into this place in front of everyone with a Colder."

Mrs M leaned closer. "Listen to me, pet. That family produced good-looking men. They were a family of shearers. I forget the name of the one who worked here years ago, but, he turned heads every time he walked down Main Street."

Her mother scoffed. "Alan's his name. That one turned heads no matter where he went."

Mrs M stroked her hair. "He's handsome, but Brock Colder is not the kind of man who will marry you, or give your mother grandchildren. A handsome man has choices all his life."

"I'm not looking for that." At least not right now.

Her mother looked across at her. "What are you looking for?"

Jen bunched her lips. Good question. At twenty-four she should know. "I'm not sure. I want to do a lot of things and don't know where to start, or how to start."

Mrs M nudged her. "Sounds like you're spoilt for choice. There are so many courses showing you how to do things. Taylah's got more cheat sheets showing her step by step of what to do; she doesn't do any of it. You don't discover anything today, you just follow the guide somebody gives you."

Her mother downed the last of her drink. "That sounds nice to be spoilt for choice. I should head off. Your father's minding JoJo tonight."

Jen laid a hand on her mother's arm. "Another drink, Mum? It's not often you get out."

Mrs M jumped up. "Come on, I'll get us another drink and then I'll take you home."

Her mother sat back, a rare smile on her face. "I'd like that."

Jen looked at the back of the room, then stood up. There was so much movement in the room with people walking across to the bar.

"He's gone, hasn't he?" asked her mother.

"He can't be far."

She searched the room and couldn't see Brock anywhere, or Gareth. Jen found it hard to believe he'd leave without letting her know and felt sure he might be in the beer garden.

"Jen, it shouldn't be your job searching for him." Her mother's voice was full of concern. "He should be seeking you out. You're that special."

She kissed her mother's cheek. "Thanks, Mum."

Jen shook her head - just when she thought her mum hardly noticed her, she comes out with a doozy and completely surprises her.

"Sorry, Mum. I can't help it, I want to find him."

Her mother shot her a warning glance. "Okay. Call us if you need to."

She smiled. "Mum, he's not an axe murderer."

"People surprise you, don't forget that."

Jen sat back and sipped her orange juice. Was that right? Did she want to find him? She certainly hadn't met any man to date who excited her on so many levels as Brock did. Could she really deny herself the chance to know him better? She certainly didn't want to change him. Chances were he would leave town without a word. In her gut she hoped not. She could recall at will every minute expression on his face just before he kissed her. She, Jennifer Rogers, had been kissed by a bad boy. And she loved it.

When she thought of that afternoon, she should be tearful, frightened and nervous. She wasn't. Jen felt something every time she saw Brock. She just couldn't nail what *it* was. A kiss was just the beginning. She shivered. She wanted so much more. He was so wrong, it frightened her.

He wasn't responsible for his family any more than she was. She couldn't change his past. She downed the last of her drink, kissed her mother goodbye.

Now, where would a bad boy go?

Chapter
Twenty-Three

B rock side-stepped around people until he caught up with Gareth who sat at the last table in the corner. He recognised the signs of his brother's anger. Gareth simmered. His brother sat upright in his chair, his chest stuck out, worked his jaw grinding his teeth, and his cold eyes flashed at him.

Gareth shot out of his chair, his movements skittish. "Outside." The low-voltage command had an undercurrent of finality. A warning.

Brock followed his brother through the throng of people around the bar. Outside, they walked to the back of the pub, toward the barbeque area where a few couples sat and chatted over a glass of wine on the wooden table and chairs.

Gareth kept moving toward the river. A light breeze picked up the closer they got to the river. Here they were hidden by the huge gum trees which lined one side of the picnic area.

His brother wanted a fight. Brock rolled up each sleeve and clenched his fists. *Go for it bro, I'm ready.*

His eyes never left his brother's face. Gareth fought a dirty fight. His meanness and cruelty were exposed during a fight.

Anger, built up over many years, blistered deep within Brock after years of being the brunt of his brother's nastiness and fisticuffs. Brock meant business and had no intention of walking away the loser. He meant to win this particular fight.

Brock moved forward, head down and tackled Gareth to the ground.

Gareth lashed out with his feet, thrashing and kicking Brock in the chest. Brock tried to keep purchase of him, but Gareth squirmed away and got back up on his feet. Brock rose and walked toward him, forcing his brother to move backwards, into the darkness, and into a small forest of trees on the banks of the river. In the moonlight Brock saw a light sheen of sweat on his brother's brow. Gareth knew he was trapped with little chance of escape. His eyes darted about searching for a way out. There was none.

Brock took a step forward. This waiting game needed to end. He lunged forward to grab his brother's shoulders. Gareth panicked and struck out, hitting him with force on his upper cheek. He swung his clenched fist and struck Brock in the chest.

End it.

With both hands Brock reached up and grabbed his brother's upper shoulders. He lifted and half dragged him to the nearest tree. He pushed Gareth against the tree, his chest heaving. Brock stared at his brother, stunned to see his lips and eyes move in unison to morph into a hideous hateful expression.

He swung at Gareth, clipping him at the bottom of his jaw. He let him go and watched his brother fall to the ground, his head just missing an exposed tree root.

He let out a breath.

After a few minutes Gareth staggered to his feet, both his hands clawing at the tree trunk to right himself. Once upright, Gareth leaned against the tree, breathing heavily. A small trickle of blood slithered down the side of his mouth.

"Brock, are you out here?"

Jen.

He stared at his brother. "That's it. Piss off," he hissed.

His brother raised his eyebrows at something past Brock's shoulder before he turned and ran further along the river bank.

Brock turned around to find Jen standing at the edge of the picnic area. She looked stunned. Her eyes roamed over his body and his gut twisted.

For years, he'd comforted himself hugging pillows as a youngster, and as an adult, sitting in the dark with a glass of red. He wanted something more; he wanted to hold onto someone, someone who meant something.

He drew in a huge breath and walked up to her. In the moonlight he caught her lovely face. She didn't look disgusted. Relief shimmied down his spine. That was a start.

He stood before her. "I'm sorry about tonight, Jen. And, I'm sorry you're not seeing me at my best."

Her eyes never wavered from his. She reached out and he fell into her arms. He held her close, drinking in her softness and smothered his head in her hair.

"Are you okay?" she whispered. "Any cuts?"

He shook his head.

"Would you like a drink out here? I'll get us a bottle of wine. It's a lovely evening."

He couldn't think of a better thing to do. It sounded so normal, but he did not live by normal. Brock eased himself away from her. "Jen, I don't think that's a good idea."

Her beautiful eyes snared him. "Why not?"

He pulled back. He'd been one hell of a fool thinking he could mix it with a local, especially one who knew his family's history. He saw the distrust in her father's eyes and he couldn't let her fall out with her family. They meant the world to her.

Brock stiffened. He didn't want to hurt her. "It's time we were honest. We come from different worlds and whatever it is between us, is only going to lead to heartache. The sooner we cut the ties before we get too involved the better."

Jen's eyes widened and he could see the hurt beginning to roll in. "How? I don't understand."

He stepped away from her before he caved in. "It's simple. I'm untested waters. I've never stayed in one place past a couple of years. I don't know how to do long term. I'm a bad bet." Brock turned and walked away. He heard her gasp and it almost fractured his resolve. He kept walking.

Chapter Twenty-Four

J en hadn't changed her routine in years. Home by six, dinner on the table, clean up after dinner, and time with JoJo followed by television. The only exception to the rule was Friday night at the pub with Taylah. Lately, Saturday night at home was the rule rather than the exception. With her parents and JoJo in Tamworth for the weekend she was free.

She needed time alone. Jen gathered together her shopping bags in readiness.

Tonight would be different. Alone. That sweet word rolled around her head. Alone to eat and do what she fancied – on the surface. Brock never left her thoughts. She was done with the sleepless nights and all the questions about why he'd walked. It hurt big time. How could two brothers be so different? Gareth was cruel, using his looks to fool her aunt.

"Will you be alright tonight? You're welcome to stay at my place if you'd like?" asked Mel as she slowed down for the sharp turn into the Rogers' property.

Jen turned to her work colleague. "Thanks, Mel, but not tonight. I'm spoiling myself."

Mel grinned. "I'm glad to hear it. What do you have planned? You got someone special coming over?" She pulled up her car as close to the verandah steps as she could get.

Jen sighed. "No, no one special, but I've got a bag load of goodies here."

Mel waved a perfectly manicured hand at her. "Don't keep it to yourself. What's in those bags?"

"No stews, rissoles or chops and three veg for me tonight. I'm going all the way with paté, different cheeses and crackers. Let me see, I've also got smoked salmon and a few slices of smoked ham."

Mel made a playful grab at her bags. "Now, I'm hungry," said Mel. "A party for one, I'm jealous."

Jen laughed as she climbed out the car. "I'm going to sip on red wine as I sup on a feast. Thanks for the lift, Mel."

Jen waved at Mel until she was out of sight.

She listened to the silence and let out a sigh. Jen knew tonight was long overdue. She craved being alone with just time to think. Laurie still hadn't mentioned making her permanent, her make-up sales weren't flash. Maybe it was time to abandon that, or start a new campaign with the newcomers moving in.

She still hadn't hinted, not even breathed a word, to her family about leaving home. Would they understand she wanted something more? First thing she did at work was to check if there was any interest in unit three. So far, it was still vacant. It couldn't stay vacant much longer.

The verandah light flashed on as she climbed the verandah steps. She cursed Laurie for keeping them back. He'd smashed her plan to have a drink and nibble watching the sun set.

Once inside, she kicked off her shoes and poured herself a glass of her favourite red, a merlot. After a few sips she headed into the bathroom for a long hot shower.

Twenty minutes later she headed back into the kitchen with an empty glass and dressed in her oldest, most comfy nightie. Asleep in front of the back door was Sam. His gentle snores mixing it with the fridge who could make the most noise.

Then she heard it.

Voices.

She paused, her head cocked toward the driveway as she listened.

Silence.

Jen pulled out a wooden platter that sat on the kitchen bench, sandwiched between the microwave and the fridge. Then she heard voices in conversation, close by. Still, she couldn't make out the words.

She rushed across to the large lounge room window and peeked through the venetian blind. Jen stared in disbelief seeing about twenty or more flash-lights walk up the driveway. She blinked. What?

As the lights approached the top of the driveway, they started to spread out. She couldn't make out what else they had in their hands beside the flash-lights. Every now and again a short, sharp light flashed.

What did they have in their hands? Her mind drew a blank as they walked ever closer to the house and she could see their forms.

Fear clutched at her throat. Men, men in black, lots of men in black were striding toward her, each with something in their hand and it looked like some metal object. Were they planning on ripping into her family home? The sheds? The old homestead?

Jen closed the blind, ran to the kitchen and switched off the one lone light she had above the cooker. The room fell into darkness. As if on auto-pilot she ran to each window in the lounge and dining rooms, locked the windows and drew the blinds.

The police. She picked up the phone handset left on the kitchen bench. It was dead. How? Who?

She ran back across to the lounge-room window. On her way Jen picked up her handbag from the lounge. From the window she watched as some men in black climbed the steps. In the car park she saw a familiar figure.

Her mouth dropped open. *No, no, no.* She watched Brock wave his arms about to disperse the men. Some went down toward the old shearing shed. Another group headed toward the old homestead.

Some ignored him and climbed the stairs leading to the verandah. Their footsteps sounded loud and solid on the floorboards and her heart pounded in her chest. Her hands fumbled, sifting through endless tissues, her hairbrush and lipsticks, for her mobile. She slipped her hands into the little pockets and drew a blank. Where was it?

Think, Jen, think.

"I'll check the house. You guys, check the paddocks." Brock's stern voice pierced through her panic and fear. *Oh, my god, does that mean he knows I'm here?* He could send anyone to check the house but he was coming himself. Her body started to shake. She clenched her hands in an effort to stop the tremors. Her mind went blank as the footsteps on the verandah receded.

The front door rattled, followed by firm solid footsteps heading to the back of the house. She heard him walk around to the back door. It too rattled when he attempted to open it.

She swallowed hard as she heard his steady steps head toward the laundry door. She wondered if her mother locked it. They never did, but they rarely left the home unattended.

Jen dropped her bag on the lounge. She heard the familiar squeak of the laundry door. Her heart sank.

She sprinted as fast as she could to the hallway, her bare feet barely touching the wooden floorboards. Jen slammed into the hallway wall and pressed her body hard against it.

Her body shook.

Chapter Twenty-Five

B rock took a step inside and switched on a light. He found himself in a laundry with neatly folded linen on the bench at the back wall; above the bench was a shelf with every conceivable washing power and liquid soap imaginable. All neat with everything in its place and not a speck of dust in sight.

He wandered into the kitchen and his senses were hit with warmth coming from the oven nearby. He checked. It was switched off. Brock took a deep breath enjoying the sudden hit of vanilla and cinnamon. He spied a home-cooked apple pie on the kitchen table and beside it a note. He read, *Enjoy the treat, Mum and Dad xx*.

An uneasy feeling grew in the pit of his stomach. What the hell was he doing here? This was a home, Jen's home. He'd visited many homes, but this was so much more than just a place to eat and sleep.

His eyes were drawn to the open bottle of red, the empty glass beside it, the packets of unopened cheeses, the paté and biscuits. His heart sank.

Brock looked past the kitchen and into the comfortable open living room. It reeked of family comforts, cushions on the lounge, a woollen rug folded neatly at one of the lounge. A bucket of soft toys and animals sat in one corner; part-way into the room was a stone wall from floor to ceiling dominated by open fireplace.

Again, all clean and tidy. He couldn't imagine how good a person could feel living in a home like this, with no half-empty bottles of beer, or empty pizza boxes lying around. This home was cared for daily, not with a weekly quick tidy-up. This was a home. He could see a woman's touch everywhere. His father had tried his best, but ... something caught his eye.

On the glass cover of a painting hanging on the stone wall a dark shadow flickered. *What is that?* He headed in the opposite direction and stepped further into the room towards the hallway. He stopped when he spied bare feet with blue painted toenails.

Brock swallowed hard. In that moment he loathed himself.

He did not sign up to terrorise anybody. This was not what he'd agreed to in order to help his brother before they went their separate ways.

What started out as a search for hidden jewels had now gone way too far. He glanced toward the darkened hallway. What now?

"Jen," he called. When she didn't answer he walked around the living area and turned on every light he could find.

At the top end of the lounge room he announced, "I won't hurt you. I'm just coming to find you."

Brock turned the corner and his heart almost broke. Jen stood trembling against the wall. Dressed in a pink nightie that fell to just above her ankles, she looked vulnerable and terrified. He reached out to touch her. She slapped his hand away. Anger flashed in her eyes. "Get away from me and get out of this house," she hissed.

He raised his hands. "Calm down."

"Now!" she screamed at him. "Go now and get those idiots off this property. Now!"

He backed away. Never in his life had he felt more at a loss at what to do next. "Calm down, Jen. You weren't meant to be here."

She stared at him, a mix of amazement and disbelief. "I wasn't meant to be here? Who told you that? This is my home. I'm meant to be here. I'll never feel safe here again."

"I'm sorry..."

"You're sorry?" she snapped. "You're lucky I couldn't find my mobile to call the police. I can't call from the landline because one of your morons has taken care of that."

"What? Nobody's tampered with your phone." He reeled at her suggestion. *Surely not one of the guys has done that? This is pure madness.*

Jen choked. "How would you know? The line is dead. Those men are uncontrollable. Who does this? What type of people are you?"

She moved away from the wall, her eyes never leaving his face. Jen's hostile questions burned into his psyche. It wasn't the first time he'd wondered what type of people they were. They were loners, wanderers who kept moving on. His gut burned. He couldn't deal with that now.

Jen stepped closer to him, swamping him with the scent of lavender, soft and alluring. Her stance gave off a different vibe. Her body stiffened, the fierceness of her gaze almost took his breath away. Jen surprised him; she possessed a toughness he didn't think existed in her. "Get out now, Brock. I won't ask again."

He shook his head. "I can't leave you like this."

"Oh, yes you can. I'll be fine."

He studied her. Brock liked what he saw. The messed pony tail atop her head and ringlets circling her neck and shoulders together with the oversized pink nightie touched him in a way he didn't understand.

Brock nodded goodbye as he walked away. He would make sure she would be fine.

Chapter Twenty-Six

Jen lay wide awake on the lounge thinking of Brock. That he was all she could think of was not surprising, considering he'd spent the whole night outside guarding her home. A couple of times he'd woken her when he'd yelled out at someone. It was probably one of those thugs returning to the property for some reason. She tossed aside the idea of asking Brock in for a coffee and breakfast. He'd burnt that bridge.

The early morning light filtered through the venetian blinds. She pulled back her blanket, slipped on her runners and grabbed her mother's cardigan from the back of her kitchen chair. She stopped at the fridge and pulled out a couple of carrots.

Jen opened the laundry door and gently closed it behind her.

Outside the air was cool. Jen walked down the small slope to the closest paddock and scanned the area. She couldn't see any damage anywhere and kept walking to the end of that paddock.

Jen stared at the old homestead. Something wasn't right, but she couldn't put her finger on it. Two of her father's horses came up for a pat and she surprised them with a carrot each. All the while her gaze kept drifting to the old homestead.

Oh, my god, why didn't I see it earlier? The front door's open. She ran down the path as fast as her legs could take her.

"Jen, hold up," called Brock.

She didn't stop, her eyes locked on the property. When she reached the corner of the building, she skidded to a halt, leapt onto the verandah and ran to the front door.

Jen stood in the doorway, stunned. She leaned against the side of the door, the scene too bizarre for her to fully comprehend. Every doll's head had been pulled off. The small lounge-room floor was full of doll's heads. She felt sick to her stomach.

Behind her she heard Brock's sharp intake of breath.

"Shit," whispered Brock.

"Precisely. Every one of those dolls has a name and every so often JoJo washes their dresses or changes their outfits. I don't believe this has happened."

Brock walked past her and picked up one of the heads.

A surge of anger rose from the depths of her belly. She was furious that strangers thought it was okay to destroy a precious part of her home. Jen rushed at Brock and pushed him away from the doll's head.

"Get out, Brock please. Leave this."

Without a word he acquiesced. She followed him out into the morning sunshine. Her head ached from lack of sleep, she was hungry, anxious and guilt ridden-that she hadn't run across to the McKenna's in the dead of night to call the police.

"I know you're after the jewels. They're not here. What did those guys carry? Guns?"

Brock pursed his lips. "No, they each had a metal detector."

"Metal detectors? Truly? Is this children's hour?"

Brock sank to sit on the verandah. "It got out of hand."

"Who does this type of thing?" she burst out. A fog cleared in her head, as the shock receded. With a clear mind her anger and frustration knew no bounds. "So you and Gareth let those oafs come here last night, into a child's room, because this is what this is, and essentially they ruin it. Are these guys your friends?"

She didn't wait for his response. Jen struggled to get her head around the sheer wanton destruction of JoJo's dolls. It was so unnecessary. "Those dolls are JoJo's and some were destined for the library to show-case them in one of their exhibits. I can't even tell you which head belongs to which doll."

"I'll fix them."

"You'll do no such thing." She snapped. Jen paced up and down the small path leading from the front door. "Why do you think *we* have the jewels?"

He looked embarrassed. She watched him; he glanced up with a wry expression on his face. "Dad said so on his death bed. They weren't told to come here. Gareth only wanted them to walk over the paddocks. He felt the jewels were buried somewhere."

Jen kept pacing and thought about that. "And that's gospel, then?"

"Doesn't everyone speak the truth on their death bed?"

Jen shook her head. "Okay. Why would they come back here? Think about it. They have a car, they've robbed a store and they have to go to Sydney. Why come back here? It doesn't make any sense. They can divvy up the funds anywhere between here and Sydney."

Brock shook his head.

An idea struck her. Jen ran up to him. "Why? Why would you come back?"

"For a woman."

Jen's mouth dropped. Was that possible? She grasped at possibilities-at JoJo receiving the yearly cards, and her suggestive smile other night. Was there a connection? Her stomach twisted at the thought. Maybe not JoJo. Maybe one of the cooks on the property at the time? She hadn't thought along the lines of love.

"Did he say that?"

Brock shook his head. "It's only a possibility, but even so, wouldn't you make plans to meet up?"

"Maybe they left something behind? Or, maybe someone held something of theirs so they had to come back and get it?"

Brock's phone buzzed. He gave it a quick glance. "Gareth's threatening to send out a search party for me. I'll head back."

Jen studied the paddocks and the horses grazing nearby. She'd always considered her home a safe haven, peaceful and loving. Right now she saw possible hiding places at the base of every tree and hollow.

"We're grasping at straws. It still leaves the main question we all want answered. Where are the jewels?"

Chapter
Twenty-Seven

J en's feet, back and arms ached and she couldn't decide
which hurt the most. After spending the afternoon
cleaning and cutting vegetables, making salads and mari-
nades, she never wanted to see another onion, lettuce, or
carrot again.

Hannah bounded into the McKenna kitchen. "Come
outside, Jen. People are arriving and it's beautiful."

Jen quickly dried her hands on a tea towel and followed
Hannah outside. It was just on dusk, her favourite time of
day.

Hannah and Taylah had spent the afternoon dressing
the verandah with fairy lights running along the awning
on each side, the table setting was all white, with white
crockery trimmed with black - it looked stunning. Given
there was only one long table, they decided that all the
men would get up and rotate their seats and leave the ladies
seated. In all it was set for great evening.

Jen leaned out over the verandah and checked the couples arriving for the barbeque. Most came prepared with

a small picnic set and blankets. Her father was playing barman tonight, later he'd start to cook the meat. Her mother walked around with a tray of canapés. She'd worn a permanent smile on her face all week and Jen wondered whether the thought of having some time to herself in the future made her a little happier. She hoped so.

Mrs M bustled past her with another tray of canapés. Taylah joined her. "Jen, both the Colder brothers have driven up. Did they win a place at the main table or the barbeque?"

"Do I have to answer that?"

Taylah laughed out now. "You just have."

Jen spied them at the top of the carpark. "Our house is unattended, they have thugs as friends, and I just wanted to keep an eye on them."

"Gotcha."

She ran down the stairs and to meet and greet. After the wettest winter in years, the paddocks were green and lush, a rare event.

Jen watched as her mother led JoJo, still dragging Cleopatra, to an old lounge in the corner on the verandah. Jen wanted her aunt where she could be seen and still be part of the festivities. It had been a stressful week keeping JoJo away from the old homestead, telling all that she knew about the night raid to Abby, and then to her parents.

Earlier Florrie had turned up with pillows, all shapes and sizes to hand out to the picnickers. JoJo happily stood alongside Florrie handing out the pillows.

As the last of the diners were seated, Jen nodded to Florrie, who clapped her hands as she walked up and down the paddock and soon all the picnickers were seated too.

She gave Florrie the thumbs up.

Jen stood at the top of the verandah stairs. She clapped her hands to get everyone's attention. She couldn't have been happier with the turn-out or how things had come together in such a short time.

At the opposite end of the main table sat Brock and Gareth, in her line of vision for most of the night.

She surveyed them all. "Welcome, everybody. We're just delighted you could all make it tonight. Please, thank the McKenna's for the use of their beautiful home tonight. We've all diced and sliced all afternoon in preparation for dinner. I want you to enjoy tonight," she glanced at the ten diners at the main table. "We'd love it if you found love, but uppermost is to have a good time. Cheers, everyone!"

She could smell the meat cooking on the barbeque and ran inside to help Mrs M and Hannah carve the meat and serve out the dinners. Her mother was already inside, preparing the desserts.

Two hours later Jen brought in the last of the dirty dishes. She kicked off her shoes.

"Have you eaten, pet?" asked Mrs M.

Jen shook her head.

"Help yourself to a chicken wing, or a meatball. They were lifesavers. I only made them for an emergency."

Jen did just that. She went inside and found trays of untouched covered food on the side board. She took a couple of meat-balls and dipped them into some barbeque sauce. She slowly munched on one as she stepped back out onto the verandah. All the diners were now sitting on the grass in the paddock chatting. It sounded nice.

Jen looked to her left, to JoJo's lounge. It was empty. She glanced across at the picnic area and couldn't see a sign of her aunt. *Where was JoJo? Where was Gareth?*

Jen ran past the carpark and stood at the top of the drive. Nobody. She ran back to the verandah steps. Her mother and Mrs M were enjoying a drink with Florrie in the paddock. Her father was cleaning up the grill. She spied Brock chatting to guests.

She ran up to her mother. "Where's JoJo?' Her mother turned to a vacant blanket on the grass and her face dropped. "She can't be far."

Jen nodded. "Okay. I'll check the stables-she might be there."

"Jen, I'll look inside," called Mrs M.

Jen's heart started to race as she ran down the narrow pathway that led to the stables. She didn't stop and ran into the stables. Inside were Hannah and Taylah checking in on the horses. They looked up. "Have you seen JoJo?"

Both shook their heads.

She ran to the end of the paddock, crawled under the fence. Now on her family's property she kept running, first toward the old homestead. Her feet pounded past the horses, she crawled under three fence lines until finally she hit the pathway to the old wooden building.

Jen didn't stop; she jumped onto the verandah and burst into the small lounge room. Her hand slid down the wall and switched on the lights. She stared in disbelief. All the dolls' heads were back on. Everything had been restored. Brock. She wandered to each room, but no JoJo.

She stood on the verandah. Where?

Then she heard it, running footsteps. They were heavy, solid. Not JoJo. She backed herself against the back-wall on the verandah and slowly walked to the edge of the verandah and peeked out.

Brock was running at full pace toward her. She stepped back into the homestead and in no time he pounded into the home behind her.

"Where's JoJo? Where's Gareth?"

He shook his head.

"You must know where he is. You're glued together," she spat out. He flinched, but she didn't care. Her anxiety grew.

"You must know. He's your brother."

Brock shook his head.

Jen took a deep breath. "Don't lie to me, Brock, please don't lie to me."

He stepped closer to her. "I'm not. I didn't even notice he'd left."

She stared at him, unsure. She questioned everything now. Her heart pounded in her chest. "When did you restore the heads?"

"That night."

His quietly spoken words reassured her, but her mother's old sayings kept haunting her with one final question. Was blood thicker than water? When it came to the crunch would he have her back?

He reached out to her, but she ran past him. *The crossroads. Somehow Gareth's lured her to the crossroads. What if...?*

He grabbed her top and pulled her back. "Jen, hold up. Gareth's angry."

She turned to Brock. "And so am I. Hand me your mobile. Mine's back at the home and I need the light, its dark out there."

Brock searched his pockets. He frowned. "I don't have it."

She stared at him in disbelief.

He held a hand up. "I'm never without it. I'll go back and call the police."

Police? He would do that?

"Ask for Senior Constable Abby Taylor. She knows what's been going on."

Brock repeated. "Abby Taylor. Okay, got it. Wait for me. Wait here and we'll search for JoJo."

"That's too long."

Brock grunted. "They won't go far. Gareth wants JoJo to show him where the jewels are. He won't be whisking her away."

She gasped. "What makes him think JoJo knows where they are?"

"I don't know."

Jen stepped closer to him. She was desperate for answers. "You must know. You talk to each other."

"He's twisted. You're no match for Gareth. If you find him, don't let him know you're there. *Promise me.*"

"Was your father having an affair with someone here?"

There was a long pause and an uneasy feeling wormed its way into her mind.

Brock's head shot up. His eyes, dark and brooding stared at her. "Do you really want the answer?"

His softly spoken words cemented her suspicions. She shook her head.

"I'll be back in five."

He left her alone, in the silence, and then she heard a roar from the crowd at the McKenna's.

"Jen," called out Brock from the darkness. "JoJo's back."

Jen ran as fast as she could back up the path. The lights were on at her home and she saw the familiar figures of her mother and Mrs M on the verandah with JoJo.

"JoJo!"

JoJo turned in her direction and waved. Her aunt stood fully clothed and dripping wet. Her mother and Mrs M stood beside her toweling her dry.

Where's Cleopatra?

Mrs M tossed the towel onto the nearest chair and grinned at her. "JoJo's been in the dam. I can't figure out why she'd be even go near there."

Jen's heart sunk. She knew why and cursed herself for being side-tracked with Gareth and Brock. She ran up to JoJo and wrapped her arms around her aunt. Her wet clothes soaked into her top. "JoJo, Are you alright?"

Her aunt nodded. Her eyes full of love and trust.

Jen took a deep breath. "Did he meet you at the crossroads? Was he there?"

Chapter
Twenty-Eight

JoJo's body stiffened and she tried to wriggle out of Jen's grasp. Her aunt's bottom lip quivered as she shook her head. One large tear drop ran down her face. "He promised," JoJo whispered. Jen's heart hitched. How dare Gareth play games with her aunt.

Damn. Where is he? Would he be in hiding at the crossroads? Did he and JoJo miss one another?

Jen took aunt's damp hand and rubbed it. "Where's Cleopatra? What did you do with her?"

JoJo shot a quick glance at Mrs M and Pam before returning to Jen. JoJo's lips curled into a cheeky grin. "Not telling, 'cause you know."

Jen hugged her aunt. *Of course!* "They're with the ones with the soft centres? Right?" Memories long forgotten shunted into position and confirmed her suspicions. She'd often been there when JoJo re-housed the jewels from doll to doll, along with saved up soft centred chocolates covered with gold wrapping. As a child she'd only been interested in the chocolates.

JoJo's face lit up with a smile.

She gave her aunt a quick peck up on the cheek. "I'll get them for you later, but we have to find him. He should have met you."

She heard voices, and saw her father walking around the side of the house with Senior Constable Abby Taylor. Jen could feel some of the tension leave her body. She looked around for Brock. *Where is he?*

She nodded to Abby. "Am I glad to see you. Gareth's missing. He was to meet up with JoJo at the crossroads, down the back here, but he wasn't there."

Abby nodded. Her sharp keen eyes taking in JoJo's appearance.

"Hello JoJo," said Abby. "We haven't met before. I'm Senior Constable Abby Taylor and Jen tells me you were meeting someone at the crossroads. Is that right?"

JoJo stared at Abby, her eyes wide with wonder. She nodded.

Abby stepped a little closer to JoJo. "Good. How did you get wet?"

JoJo's eyes flew to Jen. After a few beats JoJo shook her head.

Abby turned to Jen. "Do you have any ideas?"

"JoJo, you're not in trouble. But we need to know something. Did you go into the dam first, before you went up to the crossroads?"

JoJo gave her a long hard stare before she nodded.

"What's going on?" her mother asked.

She took the towel from her mother's hands. "Sit down for a bit, Mum. I'll say it quickly. JoJo's hidden the jewels and Gareth, Brock's brother is after them."

"Really? All this time JoJo's had them? Why?" gasped her father.

Her mother sat down, her eyes never leaving Jen's face. "I should have guessed, oh, I should have guessed JoJo would have them. I see it now. They had their eye on JoJo. All this time I thought those Colder brothers were vying for you. What a sham they are."

Jen's blood chilled at her mother's words. She'd think about her mother's words later.

Jen turned to Abby. "JoJo never goes anywhere without Cleopatra."

Abby pursed her lips, she turned and looked out over the property. She pulled out her phone and started texting.

"Right," said Abby. "Take me to the dam, we'll put the high beams on. If JoJo's turned up wet at the crossroads without Cleopatra, chances are he's probably sitting by the dam waiting for daybreak to get his hands on Cleopatra."

"I'll come too," her father said.

Abby turned. "Mr Rogers, I'm sorry, but the fewer people the better. Please stay here with your family. Jen won't be getting out of the car. I've called in Constable AJ Donaldson. He should be here soon and I've asked him to come via the private road."

Her father grimaced. "Thanks, Abby. We'll be here."

Jen slid into the car beside Abby. "The eels won't make it easy for him. The dam's full of them."

Abby started the engine. "Jen, don't try chasing either of those brothers if you see them. I just want you to direct me to the dam. We don't know if the Colder brothers are a tag team or not. Your father tells me you've become friendly with Brock Colder."

Jen sat back in the chair. "That's right. The last time I saw him he was heading to our place and was going to call the police. Did he?"

Abby nodded. "Yes, he placed the call. Any ideas where he is now?"

Jen let out a sigh. "We did arrange that after he called the police, he'd come and join me. He asked me to stick to the right side of the road, close to the bushes and make my way to the crossroads. We thought JoJo might be there waiting for Gareth. I never went."

"Okay, let's drive around the dam first."

Jen pointed towards the old homestead's roofline. "It's halfway to the homestead. Turn left at the end of this paddock."

Abby turned on the high-beams, the powerful light lit up the narrow path that led to the homestead and onto the private road. Part way down, she turned left.

Jen stared at the grey water of the dam. There was hardly a ripple. Abby slowed down the car. The bushes were thick surrounding the back of the dam. They were used as a windbreak and Abby headed straight for them.

In the distance a car horn honked. It did again.

Abby turned back to the narrow road. "There he is," Abby cried out.

Running through the bushes and headed toward the private road was Gareth. Tall and strong, he easily maneuvered his way through the bushes and undergrowth.

"You can't follow him. The paddock's fenced off."

"Right," Abby said as she steered toward the roadside. "I'll get onto the road."

Jen kept her eye on Gareth, and then he disappeared.

"I can see bushes moving. He has to climb out at the crossroads, he doesn't have a choice."

Abby drove slowly down the private road. Jen kept her eyes on the undergrowth lining the road, searching for any movement.

"There they are," cried out Abby.

Jen saw Gareth being flung out onto the centre of the road. He landed on his side and started to scramble. Climbing out of the bushes was Brock. AJ rushed up to Brock, blocking his movement. Abby parked the car and ran to Gareth. Gareth kept running and not far behind them was Brock. As they ran past AJ's car, they all ran out of sight.

Jen climbed out of the car and ran to AJ's car. In the half-moon light she saw Brock overtake Abby and continue following Gareth. She heard a yell as Brock grabbed Gareth and slammed him to the ground. She could hear Abby's voice and then silence.

Tremors ran through Jen's body. She stared in disbelief as AJ and Abby pulled the brothers apart. A few choice words floated her way from Gareth, she couldn't make out what was being said.

"Jen," called out Abby. "I told you to stay in the car. Now, please go."

Jen head jerked a nod, but couldn't move. She stood frozen to the spot as AJ frog marched Brock and Abby did the same with Gareth. Her eyes never leaving Brock.

As they drew closer to her, Jen glanced across at Brock. The man looked casual as usual, as if he didn't have a problem in the world. His face lit up in a smile. A warm rush, a lovely mix of hope and relief, flooded her body.

Satisfied, she turned and followed Abby.

"Come on, Jen. I'll take you home first. Well take them in for questioning. AJ, you take Brock. I'll take Gareth."

Once in the car, Gareth ignored her. He sat slumped in the back seat.

"Right. These jewels. Are they really in the dam? Can you get them now? Easy to get to?"

Jen didn't fancy getting into cold water, but she wanted this drama done with. "No problems. Get closer and you'll see a little platform, underneath that is a brick box which used to house a small engine. Cleopatra's in there. Do you need her tonight?"

Abby nodded. "I know it's getting late, but we need the evidence."

Hours later, as her father showered and JoJo was in bed, Jen walked down the hall to her parents' bedroom. She found her mother sitting up in bed.

Her mother grinned at her. "You going to bed soon? It's hard to sleep after the excitement of finding the money and jewels. I can't believe JoJo had them all these years."

Jen sat on the edge of the bed. "I will. Mum, Abby might come back tomorrow to ask you a few questions. Are you ready for them?"

Her mother looked stunned. "Me? What would I know?"

"Mum, please. Those shearers took the jewels and money and instead of heading straight to Sydney, they came here. Why?"

Her mother closed her eyes.

"Mum, they'd only risk it for love. What happened? You were the only one here that afternoon. All the other shearers were in town."

Jen watched her mother. Then her eyes flew up. She sniffed. "Alan Colt was like some Viking god. I'd never seen anybody like him before. He was funny, clever and a great worker. When I first saw Brock I knew what he was in town for. I knew what his father had left behind."

"Did you know JoJo had the jewels?"

Her mother shook her head. "No, I didn't. It was such a rush that day. The three of them fought trying to divvy the money up. I remember seeing dust swirls on the front road and the sirens. I knew they were being chased. They dropped the two satchels into the food trough in the shearer's shed and took off. Hours later I searched, and searched looking for those satchels and could never find them."

"So you knew all along?" asked her father. He leaned against the doorfame, his face a picture of misery.

Her mother nodded, her eyes on Jen. "Alan Colt turned JoJo's head. Like I hope Brock hasn't turned your head." Pam patted the bed. "John, it went like this. To make sure JoJo got her share from the robbery I kept their confirmation letters from the Defence Force, kind of like insurance that JoJo would get her share. They needed those letters, but when they heard the sirens, they dropped everything. I didn't have time to give them their papers."

Jen stared at her mother. "Mum, you've kept this to yourself all these years?"

Her mother pursed her lips. "Yes, JoJo and I have paid a huge price for what we agreed to do that day. I've been so afraid all these years."

Her father stepped into the room and climbed into bed. His kissed Pam on the cheek. "We have to tell Abby. I'll take you in first this in the morning."

Her mother flopped against the bedhead. "Oh, yes. Now it's out, I can't wait to tell them." She patted the bed. "Come on, Jen. There's room in here for you."

Jen crawled across the bed and slid in between her parents. Once settled between her parents, she grabbed both their hands and squeezed hard.

Chapter Twenty-Nine

"You're in," murmured Mel. "Are you okay? I thought you might take a few days off. How's your family?"

Jen could feel Mel's eyes on her as she set her bags on her desk. "All good, thanks, Mel, in fact I've never felt better."

Scotch that. For the first time in her life she was no in the mood to be messed with, and she liked it.

She switched on her PC, ran down to the kitchen and turned on the kettle, checked the fridge for fresh milk and cheese, and the cupboard for biscuits.

She ran down the hallway and checked in on Laurie. His office was empty. "Mel, what's with Laurie? He's not in."

Mel called out. "It might have something to do with the new girlfriend. Not sure. He hasn't messaged me."

Her eyes went to his wall. *Success isn't a result of spontaneous combustion. You must set yourself on fire.*

Bring it on.

She went into the compact store room, checked the stationary cupboard for paper and notepads, and as she walked out switched the printer on at the power point. Note to self: tell the cleaner not to switch off the printer.

"You might be interested," said Mel. "We had quite a few people go through unit one upstairs. We actually got some positive feedback. Fingers crossed it goes this week."

Jen sat up. That unit belonged to her. "Really? Locals? Or, were they just nosey?"

Mel scrunched her face. "All out of towners."

The back screen door slammed shut. Both Mel and Jen jumped.

Mel rolled her eyes. "He's in a mood. Have you got the kettle on?"

Jen nodded as they heard Laurie bustle down the hallway and drop his bags in his office.

"What the hell is this?" he roared. He stood in the doorway beside Jen, amazement written all over his face. "Jen? You sent me a calendar invite. Is that a mistake or a joke?"

Jen shook her head as she leaned against her desk. "No joke, Laurie."

He threw up his arms in the air. "Unbelievable," he burst out. "You know you can walk into my office anytime. It's an open door." His clear effort to try and look disgusted, annoyed and disappointed all at once was not working on her today.

Jen let out a sigh. "I tried that, Laurie but there's only one discussion I'm interested in having with you and you keep putting it off."

He stood in the doorway, staring at her with something akin to interest. Laurie shook his head, but his warm gaze met hers. "Come on then, it sounds serious."

She followed him down the hall. Never in her life had she been more prepared for a conversation.

As they seated themselves, Laurie took out a notebook. "Righto, let's make this official. You want to be made permanent. What's the date?"

"Thirty-first of October," she answered.

He eyeballed her for a moment before he wrote it down. "That's not a trick question, Jen. We've had a brilliant month and it all started with the long weekend. All that preparation worked. We should do it more often."

Her breath hitched. "We?"

He opened his drawer, pulled out an envelope and handed it to her. She stared at it before she reached out and took it. Her lips quivered in a smile and as her eyes misted over she blinked hard.

She stared at the envelope in her hands without opening it. The thick package looked official and important. She grinned at Laurie like she'd won the lottery.

"Absolutely, I want to make it we. We all work well as a team and I'm more than happy to make you permanent. In that envelope is the contract, take it home and read it. If you're happy sign it."

"Thanks, Laurie. I'll read it tonight." She let out a gentle sigh; she couldn't wait to tell her parents.

He bridged his hands under his chin. "You'll see I've also included a clause about furthering your education. I'd like you to get yourself into the real estate course at the local college. I'll pay the fees. Are you on board? I know studying is not something we've ever discussed."

Did she hear that right? "You'll pay for my tuition? Laurie, that's wonderful. Thank you. I didn't expect that at all."

He gave her a wry grin. "Call it 'investment expenditure' and I'm happy to do it." He waved his arm at her. "Now get on out of here. I had to give you a contract, we couldn't do without you. You're the only one who knows how to kick start that bloody printer."

Jen grinned to herself.

She stood up and then immediately sat back down. "Oh, and there's one more thing I need."

Laurie gave her a mock frown. "What? You're driving a hard bargain here, what is it?"

"I have an appointment with the bank at lunch to discuss my application for a home loan. I need a letter from you stating I'm permanent and what my current wages are."

He raised an eyebrow. "Oh, you are on fire today. What would you do if I hadn't given you the contract?"

"You should know. I learnt from you. I've walked these streets; you made me knock on every business in this street. I know your opposition and I know what I can offer."

Laurie's smile deepened. "Go on, Jen, get out of here. I'll do the bank letter. A loan did you say? Can I ask what for?"

She sucked in some air. "Unit three. I'd like to put in an offer. I'll do it in writing. I'm not expecting favours or anything, but I am interested."

She'd said it. The words were out there in the universe, and so was the truth. She liked the convenience of town, the early morning hot coffee hit at The Cyprus Café, the walks to the garden and parks, the closeness to the gym. Oh, she was so ready for this move, and for a place of her own.

Laurie sat back in his chair, rocking back and forth. "It's a nice little unit that one. I know it's been sitting there for a while, but people come to the country wanting rolling hills, but not all of us like to live out there, do we?"

So he agreed with her. How good is that? At some level she and Laurie saw eye to eye. In a funny sort of way, it pleased her.

"Let me see how you go with the loan, and we'll discuss a figure. Okay?"

She stood up, with a new found respect for her boss. "Thanks very much, Laurie. I appreciate the contract."

Laurie stood before her and gave her a good long stare. "People rarely surprise me, but you managed it today." He held out his hand. "Welcome aboard, Jen."

Jen shook his hand, as a charge, a thrill like she'd never experienced before possessed her. In a strange way she felt like an equal, part of a team where they all liked one another.

Clutching her contract in both hands she strode down the corridor with a sense of purpose as a surge of energy engulfed her. She did a little twirl around Mel's desk, and then twirled back to her own desk where she opened the bottom drawer and locked away her precious first contract for safekeeping before she took it home that night.

"That," she almost sang to Mel, "is my contract. I'm one important meeting down today, which went beyond my wildest dreams, and have another at lunch with the bank. I'm on fire, Mel, on fire. No more Mondayitis for me."

She sat down and clicked onto the email icon.

Mel let out a cheeky laugh. "Well, don't get too comfortable. I hate to be the one to burst your bubble, Jen, but you've got a client coming soon. Yes, he phoned ahead to make sure you were in."

"For me?"

Mel laughed. "Well, you will give out your business cards. What did you expect?"

"Right, I'm ready," said Jen as she put together a new notebook and pen. She glanced across at Laurie's sister. "Sorry, Mel. I'm going to be pain all day."

Without waiting for an answer, the doorbell rang out. Brock Colder walked in, as casual as, looking too good to be true. Her heart gave one solid throb inside her chest. The man was seriously not good for her heart health.

Mel pulled a face. "I hadn't finished telling you, but Brock called and asked to see you for five minutes. You can use the board room, it's free."

She flicked a glance at Brock. "Are you here on business?"

Brock stepped closer to her; given his size he blocked out the morning sun. "No, I'm here to see you. How are you?"

A warm charge ran over her skin at the sound of his voice. She loved how he managed to convey a subtle, but private tone that only spoke to her, even in front of Mel.

She played with the mouse and pretended to work. "I'm good, thanks. Are you okay?"

He let out a nervous cough. "I'm good, too. Can we have a private chat somewhere?"

She shook her head. "I don't think so. Mel has been privy to all my personal dramas for weeks now; you couldn't say anything that'd surprise her. So, let's start again. If you're staying, are you looking for something to buy or lease?"

He sat on the corner of her desk. His warm ginger spicy aftershave lingered wherever he moved and she loved every breath of it.

"Jen, look at me, please. I need a minute."

"A minute," scoffed Mel. "I'll go and make some coffee."

"Jen, please, I'm staying with Reg until things settle. I'm only here with one thing in mind."

She glanced up at him. His handsome face still bore the cuts and some faded bruises of his fight with Gareth, but he looked well. Her fingers itched to run a hand over the bruise above his eye, to ruffle his hair, to see how he was travelling.

"What?" she asked.

Brock fiddled with his shirt. She watched, with only the ticking clock on the wall opposite breaking the silence. His face broke out into a nervous unsure half-smile. Something inside her bloomed at seeing his unease.

He leaned closer, his handsome face a couple of inches from hers. "I wanted to ask you out. I want to take you somewhere nice for dinner and get to know you. I think it's time."

She swallowed hard. Jen closed her eyes. It would be so tempting to rush in and say, yes, but they had a history and during all of it he'd done his best to protect her. In truth, she couldn't ask for more. Still, she knew better than most the cost of rushing in.

"For God's sake, woman," bellowed Laurie. "Don't keep the man waiting."

Jen's eyes flew open and saw Laurie and Mel, grinning like they didn't have a care in the world, standing crowded together in the doorway.

"Will those in the gallery please keep quiet. A girl's got to be sure. We have a certain history between us."

"Carry on," said Laurie.

Jen faced Brock; she was so close she could see in places where his blue eyes, were the palest of blue. "Why?"

He blushed. His blush was almost her undoing. "You make me feel good."

She grimaced. "A cold beer can do that. Why?"

"I like you, Jen. I like you a real lot."

She reached out and touched his brow. "You're sweating? Are you alright?"

He wiped his brow with the back of his hand. "You would be too. Asking you out is a big deal for me. I haven't lived anywhere longer than eighteen months in my life and I like living here in Bindarra Creek. It feels nice to find a place to put down my tackle and stay."

Her heart swelled and she couldn't hold back any-more. She ran her fingers down the side of his face and took his face in her hands. "The answer is yes. Yes, I'd love to go out with you."

"Woo hoo," said Mel. "Well, don't mind us, but that's the best news I've heard all week."

"Nice to see you again, Brock," shot back Laurie.

Jen burst out laughing. "It can't get any better can it?"

Brock grinned at her and then something to her left caught his eye. "What? No jellybeans?"

Jen shook her head. "It's not very professional."

He tweaked her nose. "Hang on a bit." He broke away from her and ran out of the agency.

"Where is he going?" asked Laurie.

"What happened there?" asked Mel.

Jen ran across to the glass door and looked out. Main Street was busy for a Monday morning with a queue outside the bank. The post office looked packed as well. With the heavy traffic going past it took a while before she spotted Brock rush into the local food store a block away on the street opposite.

"Oh, look. There's Brock. Oh, how romantic. Don't let him go, Jen," clapped Mel.

"Oh, that man puts us all to shame," grumbled Laurie.

Brock stood outside the food store waiting for a break in the traffic. In his arms was a gorgeous bunch of white flowers. He held them awkwardly, as if frightened they'd break or crumble.

"Give me five, Laurie."

She didn't wait for his answer; she rushed out the door and waved to Brock. He saw her and in the next break in traffic, he ran across to her.

"They're gorgeous. What are they?"

"Sweetpeas, I had to get them for you."

She took the delicate flowers from him; he looked big and awkward with them in his arms. She loved him for it. Yes, loved him.

His face broke out into the widest smile. "It's a big day. You said yes. After all that's happened between us, you said yes."

His sincerity caught at her throat. A hit of emotion so strong rocked her. She reached out with her free arm and drew him to her. Jen wanted to sink inside his skin if she could, and never leave.

He dropped his head and his lips gently brushed hers. Her world shifted on its axis at his tenderness; she pressed herself closer and his kiss deepened.

She could hear the cheers and hand clapping. Jen ignored them all and didn't break away. They'd each found their own gem in one other.

'The End

Thank you so much for taking the time to read my story, **_Only She Knew_**, which is part of the group writing venture – A Bindarra Creek Mystery Romance Series

All reviews are appreciated.

Word of mouth recommendations have given me many wonderful books to enjoy and I'd love it if you tell friends if you have enjoyed Jen and Brock's story.

For your reading pleasure, here is an excerpt from the next book in the Bindarra Creek Mystery Romance Series:

Secrets of River Cottage © Annie Seaton

Cathy Kendall stood at the doorway of River Cottage and tried to stay calm. For once, the gentle burbling of the river across the paddock failed to calm her turbulent thoughts. There was no way she could live in this house again.

No way.

The memories, the fear, and the expectation that her past would finally catch up with her turned her blood to ice. She closed her eyes and took a deep breath as a hand tugged at her arm.

'Mum, this is way cool,' Billy, her twelve-year-old son's voice was filled with excitement. 'I can fish all day.'

'You'll be at school all day,' Cathy said as she turned away from the door. 'Anyway, it's not certain we'll be living here yet, so don't get too excited. There's a lot to be decided.'

'Maybe we can go and live at the beach with Nan and Pa, Mummy,' Josie said. 'I don't want them to move away.'

'Aw, come on Mum.' As usual, Billy persisted. 'If we live here, I can fish after school. We can eat what I catch. It would save us some money.'

Josie's little hand snuck into hers. 'It would be a nice house to live in. Look at that stove.' Her daughter was intuitive and had picked up on Cathy's mood, as she always did.

Cathy turned reluctantly to the old combustion stove, and her hand tingled from the memory of an accident a long time ago.

No, it hadn't been an accident. She pushed the thought away as her hand seemed to burn all over again.

'We can bake all sorts of cakes. Do you think it would be all right for sponges?' Her ten-year-old daughter had inherited Cathy's love of baking. 'And there might be duck eggs here too. I saw some ducks at the pond when we drove in. If there are, that would be the absolute icing on the cake!'

Cathy's lips tilted in a smile as Josie parroted one of her nan's sayings. 'It would be, wouldn't it sweetie? "The icing on the cake" indeed.'

She looked around the kitchen, telling herself it was only a building. Bricks and mortar, or in this case, half rotten weatherboards and a rusty roof. Cathy knew she had to put her children first and leave the past behind. The memories weren't embedded in the building; they were in her mind and they would follow her wherever they lived. It was time to let go of the past, and the move away from Russ's family would be the catalyst for starting afresh, even if they were in Bindarra Creek.

Russ wasn't here, and he wasn't coming back; that was one of the few certainties in her life. When her in-laws, David and Lea, had announced they were retiring to the coast, Cathy had no inkling that she and the children would have to leave the farm. They'd lived there since Russ had left, and it was the only home Billy and Josie knew. When David told her Jon and Cleo were moving in to take over the property, Cathy had panicked.

'Oh, sweetheart.' Lea's work-roughened hand had taken Cathy's as she widened her eyes and stared. She knew the colour had left her face by Lea's stricken expression. 'Oh, we've handled this all wrong. We'd never abandon you, Cathy. You know you're like a daughter to us,' her mother-in-law said. The words that always remained unspoken hung in the air.

Like our son did.

'It's good news and it's exciting for you all. We're going to do up River Cottage for you to live in. So much better for Billy and Josie to be in town. They can go to after-school activities, and they won't have that bus trip to town every day.'

'And Mum?' Billy's voice pulled Cathy from her thoughts. 'I can get a kayak and go kayaking across the road with Eddie.'

Cathy frowned. 'Eddie? Who's Eddie?'

'You know, Mum! Eddie Taylor. He's in year eight.'

Cathy nodded. 'Oh yes, Abby and Roman's youngest. I didn't know he was one of your friends.'

'He hangs with us at lunchtime because some of the year eight boys were bullying him about his dad not being his real dad. But I stood up for him. At least, he's got a dad to do things with.'

Guilt pierced Cathy's chest, but before she could answer Billy kept talking.

'Anyway, Mum. He's always telling me how much fun it is, and he's invited me out there one day to go for a paddle.'

Cathy frowned. 'Oh, I don't know about that, Billy. That river can be dangerous.'

'Aw, Mum. I can wear a life jacket and anyway, Eddie's dad's in the SES. And now it's getting warmer I can do swimming lessons at the pool. Especially if we're in town. I could go every afternoon.'

Cathy straightened and folded her arms. 'There's a lot to be decided before we start talking swimming lessons and kayaking. This old place needs a lot of work even if we do decide to live here. It's been empty for a long time.'

'Why, Mummy? Is it a bad house? Is that why no one wants to live here?' Josie's face crumpled in a frown, and Cathy crouched in front of her. Her daughter was small for her age, and along with her intuition came a lot of worry. She was a sensitive little soul, and, like Billy, always took on the more needy children as her friends at school. Cathy had tried to shield her children as best she could—depending on who you listened to over the years, the town gossip had had Russ in jail, running away with a bikie gang, and living the high life in Bali.

'No sweetie, it's Nan and Pa's house in town, and they didn't ever rent it out. It's got a bit old, but Pa said they are going to do it up for us if we decide to live here.'

'Please, please, please, Mum.' Billy danced around her. 'You could do canteen at school, and we could go for walks along the river, and lots and lots of good things.'

Cathy forced a smile to her face; she couldn't put the inspection off any longer. 'Come on, let's go and look at the rest of the house and we can think about it. We have plenty of time. Nana and Pa aren't going to the coast until next year.

##

As they turned into the driveway that led to the Kendall farmhouse nestled in the foothills of the Great Dividing Range—not as far out of town as Billy declared—Cathy was surprised to see Jon and Cleo's ute parked near the shed. As far as she knew, they were up north visiting Cleo's parents on their cane farm in North Queensland while Cleo could still fly. Their new baby was due at Christmas.

Cleo was sitting in the sun in the front garden as they opened the gate. One-year-old Benjamin came tottering towards them.

'Oh, Benny's walking. Mum, look!' Josie raced over and held her cousin's hand. 'Clever Benny!'

'Hi Cleo,' Cathy said. 'Is everything okay? You're back early.'

Cleo reached up and ran a hand through her blonde curls. 'Hi, Cathy. Everything's fine, but there's been a slight change in plans. I'll let Lea and David fill you in. What was River Cottage like?'

Cathy put her bag on the table and sat in the chair opposite Cleo. 'Actually, it was nowhere near as bad as I expected. Lea's hired Bridie Bentley to clean it once a month apparently.'

'I thought Bridie left town to live with her daughter after all that stuff out at the Bentley farm a few months ago.'

'No, she seems to have a lot more confidence these days. You see her around town often now.' Cathy laughed. 'Not that I'm in there that often. I've run into her a few times and she told me Lea has her doing the cleaning. The house is old, but it's liveable.'

'That's good.'

Cathy sent a shrewd glance in Cleo's direction. 'Why do you say that?'

Cleo waved her hand, but a flush stained her fair cheeks. 'Come in, and we'll let David and Lea tell you what's going on.'

Half an hour later, Cathy put her teacup on the table and forced a bright note into her voice. Billy had gone out with David to feed the poddy calf, and Lea was peeling vegetables for dinner. Cleo had taken Benny to the spare room for them both to have a rest.

'So, two weeks, Lea?'

'Yes, and I have so much to do, I don't know where to start.'

'I'll give you a hand. Just tell me anything I can do to help.'

'I still haven't got my head around David changing our plans. When the house sitters let us know they had to leave, he jumped at the chance of moving early.' Lea shook her head. 'I've got so much on, and it's not long until Christmas. Now I've got to pack up the house and move to Nambucca Heads in two weeks.' She pulled out the chair opposite Cathy and picked up the teapot. 'A top-up?'

'Yes, please.' Cathy was still in shock. Once David had explained what was going on, he had asked if she was happy to move into town with the children at the same time. As Billy and Josie looked up at her with gleeful anticipation on their faces, she found herself nodding.

As well as helping Lea pack up, she had to get herself organised. Not that they really had that much of their own to pack.

'David is going to ring Dodge to take a look at the cottage, and while he's there, you could talk to Dodge about furniture. He and Tessa are just back from a trip out west with a truckload of furniture from garage sales. I heard they're having a sale to make room in their shop. You might pick up some pieces for the house. If you see anything, we'll pay for it.'

Cathy shook her head. 'No, Lea. It's about time I stood on my own two feet. You and David took us in when Russ left, and you've been incredibly good to us. I need to make a home for Billy and Josie. I've been thinking of picking up some more hours in town, and Jaclyn said there's a full-time clerical job coming up at the high school. She finished her maternity leave after Christmas, and I know I'd have a good chance of getting the job.' Cathy smiled. 'You left big shoes to fill there, Lea. Jaclyn said you spoiled her for anyone else.'

Lea's eyes glinted with unshed tears. 'You don't have to work, you know that, Cathy. It was our son who let you down so badly and looking after you and the kids financially is the least we can do.'

Cathy reached out and touched her mother-in-law's hand. 'Lea, you've done it for long enough. I need to learn to stand on my own two feet.'

'I just wish we knew what happened to him. Is my Russ still alive? I guess I have to accept he's not, because if he was, he couldn't have stayed away, could he?' Tears were rolling down Lea's cheeks now.

Cathy gripped her hand. 'Come on, let's think about something happy. You don't want to end up with a migraine.'

Lea smiled through her tears. 'I certainly don't have time for that.'

As Cathy searched for a happier topic, Josie came in from the sunroom where she'd been reading.

'Don't cry, Nan. Like Mummy said, let's think about something good. Let's talk about Aunty Cleo's new baby. She let me feel her kick in her tummy before.'

Lea held her arms out and Josie sat on her lap, her little fingers wiping Lea's cheeks. 'And Aunty Cleo asked me for some ideas for our new baby's name too.'

Cathy smiled at her daughter as she looked across at her. In less than a minute, Josie had Lea smiling and distracted.

But what could you say to a mother whose child had disappeared of his own accord? Cathy couldn't imagine what that would be like. She prayed that neither of the children had Russ's temperament.

There was so much that Lea didn't know about her son. And Cathy would never tell her.

***

BUY NOW

A Bindarra Creek Mystery Romance Series – released from July 2022

Amulet of Death – Suzanne Gilchrist (aka S.E . Gilchrist)

Beyond the Gate – Rhonda Forrest

Protecting Their Destiny – Erin Moira O'Hara
Only She Knew – Linda Charles
Secrets of River Cottage – Annie Seaton
Forgotten Secrets – Susanne Bellamy
A   Perfect   Danger   –   Phillipa   Nefri
Clark

About the Bindarra Creek Series

Wecome to Bindarra Creek, a struggling country town where people work hard and love deeply. Set in the picturesque tablelands of New England, Australia, Bindarra Creek is a fictional, rural community full of romance, intrigue, adventure, drama and suspense.

To date there are four multi-author 'series' set in the Bindarra Creek world all written by best-selling Australian romance authors. A fifth is planned for late 2022 – A Bindarra Creek Christmas.

Bindarra Creek A Town Reborn

Take Me Home – Suzanne Gilchrist (aka S E Gilchrist)
In the Heat of the Night – Susanne Bellamy
No Looking Back - Linda Charles
Worth the Wait – Annie Seaton
With Every Breath – Lauren K. McKellar
Stealing Her Heart – Simone Angela
A Twist of Fate – Erin Moira O'Hara
Promise Me Forever – Juanita Kees

Bindarra Creek Short & Sweet

What's in a Kiss? – Linda Charles
My Forever Valentine – Sandie James (not available)

Pearls and Green Beer – Susanne Bellamy

Full Circle – Annie Seaton

Date with Destiny – Erin Moira O'Hara

A Letter From the Queen – Lee Christine

Love's Sweet Challenge – Suzanne Gilchrist (aka S E Gilchrist)

The Widow Maker – Lauren K. McKellar

Out of the Blue – Noelle Clark

Bindarra Creek Romance

Bindarra Creek Makeover - S. E. Gilchrist

Shadows of the Heart - Lee Christine

Second Chance Love - Susanne Bellamy

The CEO Mechanic - Sandie James (not available)

Reach for the Stars - Kerrie Paterson

Home to Bindarra Creek - Juanita Kees

Stolen Sanctuary - Stacey Nash

Tempting Fate - Erin Moira O'Hara

One More Day - Linda Charles

The Vine - Lauren K. McKellar

The Ghost of His Past - Simone Angela

Joanie's Dilemma - Marianne Theresa

Buckley's Chance - Noelle Clark

Full details on buy links for all books in Bindarra Creek world can be found at: www.bindarracreekromance.com

About Author

Linda Charles is a contemporary romance writer who lives in Newcastle in the Hunter Valley, NSW. She was born and raised in Sydney where she studied and taught drama for many years. She loves to read, travel and enjoys a good conversation. Following a move to the Hunter Valley she started to write her own stories. Her new year plans always include getting fit enough to enjoy a walking holiday in the outback.

You can visit Linda at her Webpage
www.lindacharles.com.au